To: Andy
From: Mike
This book will r
Enjoy!

CRUISIN' AROUND "SAY-TOWN"

CRUISIN' AROUND "SAY-TOWN"

Mike Mullins

iUniverse, Inc.
New York Lincoln Shanghai

Cruisin' Around "Say-Town"

iUniverse books may be ordered through booksellers or by contacting:

iUniverse
2021 Pine Lake Road, Suite 100
Lincoln, NE 68512
www.iuniverse.com
1-800-Authors (1-800-288-4677)

Because of the dynamic nature of the Internet, any Web addresses or links contained in this book may have changed since publication and may no longer be valid.

This is a work of fiction. All of the characters, names, incidents, organizations, and dialogue in this novel are either the products of the author's imagination or are used fictitiously.

ISBN: 978-0-595-47669-5 (pbk)
ISBN: 978-0-595-91934-5 (ebk)

Printed in the United States of America

I dedicate this book to all my friends and family, especially those that have shown interest in my writing over the years. I honor two teachers I consider mentors, Robert Bain, English teacher at Central Catholic High School in San Antonio, Texas, and James Kelman, world renowned author and a person who believed in my writing potential early on. Finally, I want to thank all those actual human beings on whom characters in my book are based. Love you or hate you, you provided my material. Thank you.

BOOK I:

DR. JONES

CHAPTER 1

▼

You know how it is. It's good, it's bad, it's everything. When you know the people I now know, there's no such thing as fear. Fear won't exist, fear can't exist. All you can do is move forward, no matter what tragedy may strike. I will defend those girls, defend them until the end. Because I have to. There's no choice. Because you either solve the problem or cause the problem. There is no safe middle ground. Middle ground is the most dangerous place. That's what you have to do. Just cruise around Say-Town one night and the truth will be revealed to you.

*   *   *   *

I met him in a dark corner alley of my house. A house that from the outside looks like pain. Dull, tan pain(the brick color.) A hatred so pervasive it's not even there. You get used to it. Or so you think. How can you know unless you were actually there? Smack dab in the middle of the Sampson High School area, there was an enveloping yet illusory peace. Until the FBI came. Not to us but to charge across the street. Me looking then running to my room like a scared child unfamiliar with benign disguises on Halloween. But no benignity exists in an FBI raid. On either side. Shoot first, ask questions later. That's what they always say. But how do you ask questions to a dead man? You don't You just look down and smile because you have won. But only a battle, not the war. Especially a war that will never end.

I think this as I snuggle in my bed in the middle of the afternoon, a sick kindergartner but not sucking my thumb, thinking I had to hold on to some vestige of adulthood. How can I be a man and act like this? Shouldn't I confront them?

Sure. Get shot or arrested so I could help out my "homies?" Turns out they weren't even there. The only one murdered was the pit bull who could not keep his mouth shut. What, the dog out of line for barking? He was defending his owner's house. In another life, he could have actually worked for the Feds. Maybe in his next life he'll be a seeing eye dog, if it befits his breed. That gives me even less reason to think I'll be a hero for a lost cause. My only connection to these neighbors is the dog they gave us. The sweetest dog in the world, Layla. But even her love could not temper our house of hate. Nothing could. She left a house of worst to a house of not as bad, but bad nonetheless. Layla didn't seem to understand pain, division or hate as most dogs do. Now that she's gone(stolen from us), sometimes I think she was a queen on a throne from another realm, sent by a king who saw our world and wanted to improve it, not take it over. This sounds strange, but I don't know how this other realm thinks. Do they actually look out for their fellow men(or creatures)? I didn't know then and I don't know now. What I do know is in my world, the cream rises to the top and compassion sinks lower than any container can hold, under the weight of cowardly feet that can only gain strength in numbers.

✳   ✳   ✳   ✳

My new associate and I soon took to the streets. He had to show me his world, a world literally across the tracks from the neighborhood in which I grew up. He made me know his world. I did not want to know it. But it was important to him. I grew to accept it, grudgingly. But never totally. I wasn't afraid, but I was not at ease. But then I am not at ease with anyone, anywhere, anytime. But that is not a phobia. It is a mislike and mistrust against the entire human race. You never know when someone will screw you. Even your close confidants.

But I had to trust my new associate. Riches and fame, maybe. Street cred, definitely. But I had to do my part, not sit like a bump on a log. I had become a hero to my city, my hometown, "Say-Town." The gladiatorial police force but not a cop by any means. I was only protecting the interests of me and my friends. The mob does that. Some of them thought I was a Narc. It was nothing more than putting a mark on a marked man. I don't care I am not going to do their drugs or play their games, especially with sex. I have to hang around this corruption to protect the women involved. All of them. Even Precious.

Precious is a story unto herself. Ever since she had come along, she has done nothing but rock the boat. In my eyes she is the smartest, stupidest, classiest, sexiest, most disgusting creature on this planet. She represented to me the type of dilemma that only the strongest of men can resist.

I fell for it. I tried to be her man but she didn't want me. Told me I didn't talk about her enough. There's a reason. I just wasn't interested in anything about her. Yet I wanted her. She dangled little carrots in front of me, with all her, "I love yous" and fondlings.

To paraphrase my associate, what a stupid-ass trick. Lots of tricks, few treats. She was willing to have sex with almost any man she met(expect me). She claimed I didn't respect her even though I did. I guarantee you none of those other men respected her. It was the old, "Nice guys left to pasture," and I'm not even that nice. But I had begun to hate her, and I hoped I would soon be able to forget how much I wanted her.

*   *   *   *

My associate always makes me go with him. That's how you become a professional. A professional gets work done in the most dire of circumstances.

My partner can sit in a loud house with drugs and not even flinch. I need quiet and more quiet. Even classical music makes me think off task. Suddenly I am thinking of Bach and Beethoven and Amadeus and realize they have way more talent than me. I always developed my talent, given none and forced to work. My "best friend" bailed on the dream. He wanted to write, then gave up. He's a natural born writer. Better than me. But if it makes him happy, he can sit in the courthouse and raise his family, living the American tax payer's dream. He might say, "I want my house, I want my fence, I want my kids. I want sex with my wife at least once a week and basketball another once a week. Drink Budweiser and watch Bruckheimer movies, lounging in my perfect world with no temptations and no problems. Even Mookie can come over after awhile, after I'm comfortable with him, but that will take awhile. First I have to start my family and then everything will fall into place."

That, of course, was a crude summary, but at least a little accurate. I look through a route of life that is winding and unpredictable yet at times I want to plan it out like Cody's. No more stress, no more mental illness and aggravation, only togetherness with those in the same boat as me.

✳   ✳   ✳   ✳

I want to surround myself with the "weak people" because I am a weak person as well. There are two types of people in this world. Victims and victimizers. The victimizers party at the former's expense, thinking it will never end. But it will. Eventually the victims will arise from underfoot and assert an authority they never had. Once this happens, the Victimizers grasp at straws to overhaul their victim friends again, pleading with gifts and apologies, hat in hand, creating a new world for you that cannot possibly exist. You finally realize, why would things change?

It's as if 30 poisonous snakes surrounded you with flirty eyes and slithering dance moves after trying to venom your throat the night before. How can it possibly change that soon? How can it possibly change at all? It can't and you know that. But you hope. You hope for the kind of change in a scoundrel that is damn near impossible. But that's the problem. You think "damn near" instead of totally. You need to shut out those venom pushers, even if the venom feels sweet. Run away if you have to, there's no cowardice in that.

But I know C.M. spreads no venom at least not to me. He's more of a garden snake, the kind of creature that looks scary but will not bite. At least, this is what I thought at first. And one thing he can do is create an image, looking like an anaconda, terrifying people while he smiles at them.

When he walks into a high school, administration clears. I walked into one with him and watched how the VP and others darted into their offices, clutching their walkies like in the Vietnam War. Those people create the wars, not the pedestrians walking through the war zone. You lose your inhibitions, you lose your fears. What, is a fucking 17 year old going to jump on my back? If he does, my compadre will rip to the ground and choke him with his foot. So, does the real snake come out when necessary? One thing I know is I have to be ready if this happens. At first, all I knew was the stories of what he told and he told me how he talked when someone fucked with him. You know, so back at the high school as he throttles the student, he says, "You wanna get up, motherfucker? It's e-e-e-easy." And he would draw it out just like that. Before you know it, this kick ass kid is shitting bricks. We just created a new secondary sport. It's called, "Take on the grown-ups." You think you're bad? Just step up to Mr. C.M., Mr. Rock Your World." He'll head butt you, kick you in the balls, whatever it takes to get you on the ground and throttle you. You can back out at any time but once you bring it, it's waaaay to late.(Again, C.M. speak)

Also, if you back out, you are a pussy. The biggest pussy who ever lived. So it's your choice, either floor putty or school pussy. 9 times out of 10 they take the pussy route and that 10th will be pummeled. Don't mess with us. You don't know our world. No one will, yet it's there and no one will get us. Me and C.M., rockers supreme, Say-Town magnificent, rulers of a realm far from heaven yet above the depths of hell. I'll look Satan in his green eyes every time and not flinch because God's got my back, a person more powerful than C.M. can possibly imagine.

*   *   *   *

I want to know more about the people of this world, their inner intentions good and bad. Good and evil are so intertwined in every day life it is very difficult to draw that line in the sand between acceptable and unacceptable evil. I drink and smoke cigarettes. So what?

Compared to everyone else in this group, I am a monk. That's why they are suspicious of me. It's as if they're saying, "He's not part of the team. Let's keep our eyes on him. What am I s'posed to do, snort a line and go maniacally roaming the city like a Jesus Christ without the Disciples? I may think I can make extra food but I can't. I can go buy some food. I have ten dollars in my pocket. But I don't want to feed all those motherfuckers. I want to feed some of them, only the ones I like. But I know what'll happen if I do that. The others whom I don't like will be all, "What about me? I let you chill here all the time. I provided you a lot more than 10 dollars."

So instead of my noble mission, I acquiesce to the "We are the World" pipe dream. And for a night it works. Everyone is fed and happy and M. Jones is the greatest guy on the face of the earth. Until tomorrow when all is forgotten except, "What have you done for me lately? Get out of my house, you ungrateful prick. I let you stay here for two days, you didn't buy groceries, ate my food, talked to my women, watched my DVDs, listened to my CDs, jammed out to my turntables, smoked in my house. Get out and don't come back."

Yet he never tells the girls that. They're damned or they're damned. Get out, don't leave. Get out, don't leave. It's a circus of the absurd. "Ladies and gentlemen, let me introduce you to the slave girls. I lure them here, them I keep them here. The power is in my mind and I control them with money and empty promises. I load them in a beautiful woman clown car, complete with leather seats and blaring stereo. You know they get wet to that techno. That's why I play it. I don't even like it myself . But I do it for the ladies. It's like fishing in a shallow pond. I will get mine. I can fuck them whenever I want or just fuck them over whenever I want. My male friends are a different story. As long as I get my money, everything's cool. Otherwise, no. That's just the way it is."

Mr. Shystee McKracken is the purveyor of most of these sins. Money is his God. Other than investments and bank accounts, he piles a whole stash of cash under his mattress. That's his life insurance for such things as flood or friend insurance. He always knows he can buy his friends back or anyone else for that matter. Every night before he goes to bed, he lifts it up and counts his remaining dreams. I say remaining because a little bit gets taken at a time, the cost needed to maintain his control. But he can always get more from his parents. The ones who bought him the house and that beautiful, too friendly dog.

I like his dog more than he does. But then I'm a dog lover and he's just a hater of living beings. Because he loves money. And no matter how much people hate him, his money never will because, after all, it gave them those drugs, those friends, those women. So he owes money. But how can one possibly pay money back to money itself? By doing what it tells you to. But it's for your own good, so don't question it. Just enjoy the feast. Because when those people leave you, money will always be there. Under your mattress. Looking after you. Making sure everything is okay. Just think of money when you are trying to sleep and it will sing a lullaby and promise to make things better in the morning. Say hello to Mr. Shystee McKracken, all for he and he for none, sheltered by money, money his one true friend.

*   *   *   *

Every day, I prefer to do the driving. At least then I know exactly where I'm going. I get in C.M.'s car and he goes, "You'll see nigga." But I don't want to know then, I want to know now. It seems like the only time I'm in control is when I'm behind the wheel. My music, my speed, my destiny. My destination is not always positive, But is usually necessary.

I don't care if I'm going to the store or the opera, my human transactions at either are important. Do I want to see a white faced fat lady hit those notes or a brown faced cutie drone out numbers? Everything has a trade off. The opera lady is unattractive and the store girl is uninteresting. Mental stimulation versus a hot chick in bed. For one thing I don't understand the language opera lady sings and store girl will reject my advances.

But there is one word that counteracts this law. Serendipity. Serendipity is some good results that happens to you beyond any possible expectations. Store girl doesn't just flirt with me, she goes on break, drags me into the corner of the break room and fucks my brains out. To her it's like a fucking smoke break. To me, it's sex of a lifetime. What about the opera lady? Get her autograph? I certainly don't want to fuck her. Or her friends. But maybe I land the gig of a lifetime. Get to be the male lead in the next production. Because I can sing and cake my face in makeup.

Tour the country as a troubadour extreme. Then I'm signing the autographs. Before you know it, I'm hitting it with all the hot opera groupies. You'd be surprised, they exist. So by this rationale, the opera version looks like the better alternative but is much less likely. One quick dalliance with the store employee, or tons of nookie on the opera circuit after much hard jumping through hoops and being on display. Tade offs.

Same with my car versus C.M.'s car. Adventure vs. safety. Part of me is the five year old saying, "Yeah, we get to go for a ride." Part of me is the rational, world hardened twenty-something who cares less for lust of adventure and more for his soft couch and comedy reruns.

Smoking softens my anxiety and somehow my lust. And lust can lead to anxiety, especially when you aren't getting any and everyone else is. But I need to get off that. It is a destructive behavior and looks bad in front of other people. And I need to maintain my rep. It took me twenty something years to attain it and there is no way I'm giving it up now.

I know I am on a high soapbox rather often, but I am better than everyone else. I am not even exaggerating. I have to be better than everyone else. Because I can't be worse. Like my brother always says to me, "One extreme or the other, M." I love extremes. Extremes are what make chocolate chocolate and vanilla vanilla. Everyone loves chocolate but what the hell is wrong with vanilla? Vanilla is chill time and chocolate is clubbing time. Bump Bump Bump. Get my grind on. Get my groove on. Whatever chick I see lay (or more accurately dance) ahead is nothing but warm putty in my delicious chocolate hands. I'm not black and I didn't just smear my palms in ice cream. It's the spirit of the flavor. It's go time. If you have a chocolate mind, your id rises and your superego subsides. The id feeds off the chocolate intake of your successes and experiences.

But you had better be careful. I have to be careful. I have known superheroes who toppled from their heights when faced with chocolate overdose.

Chocolate overdose occurs when one soaks up the lust of power and pats on the back from their fellow men. Those insidious pats contribute to the overdose, but if you are so great and better than everyone, you should be able to temper the praise. In fact, there is no reason you shouldn't know better. When it seems too good to be true, it is. Not it probably is, but it is. It's guaranteed. So with a riddle that to me at least is so easily solvable, why do so many great men fall into this insidious trap?

Because their heads explode with the chocolate buildup. Shouldn't they know that their bodies and spirits need a balanced diet? The Zone Diet makes you motionless and the Atkins Diet gives you heart attacks.

The chocolate extreme carries you to fantasy world. 'Sweet, sweet chocolate. All day, all night. Everything's always perfect. Everybody loves me. Everybody fears me. I got enough money. I got a kick ass chick who likes to fuck all the time. I am an immortal. An untouchable. I am always right, therefore I am never wrong. The sum results of all my deeds is equally the inverse of any other's attempt to get the better of me. Because it can't be done."

Listen to Mr. Egomaniac. These flavored infusions left him with choclate brain clots. Not physically fatal but certainly spiritually so.

It will catch up to him. It will. Because after a while, people see through the bullshit to the pulsating id monster who now runs the show. The head cheerleader will leave the star quarterback for the valedictorian.

Because the head cheerleader is actually smart enough to hang with Mr. Calculator. See how the tables have turned? He knew in high school that there was no way on God's green earth that he would ever get with her.

But he accepted his lot in life. He loved to dream, but often his dreams scoured many different paths, kind if spreading a paint brush over the whole horizon of futures.

This approach was actually very practical. Mr. Calculator typed it in to his mini super computer to achieve the desired results. "Schoolwork+club activities=energy+high class rank+SAT+top university." He chose the nerd route, studying so many Friday nights rather than partake in Clothes+Party=Sex+Drugs+Rock'n'Roll. The decadent cliché. The word decadent means exactly what it says. Somehow during the '80s or something it got flipped around to mean something positive. Ergo: The decadence of Motley Crue's lifestyle led to sex with any girls they wanted and free drugs. "Weeeee! I'm flying down the highway at three in the morning. Heroin smoothes mountains into hills. Who gives a fuck about that fat bitch anyway? She told me, "Drive my car and I will fuck you. Or was it the other way around? I don't remember. It doesn't matter. I'm driving up the coast to San Francisco tonight. I'll live in a fucking town house till kingdom come. Fuck the band. I'll put my own band together, call it the Anti-Fairie Force. I'll cruise through the hilly streets in this very car, the one I stole, a successful thievery backed by those who support my mission. I don't want to eliminate fags, just control them You know, keep their numbers closer to the 10% that they're supposed to be.

"Jesus Christ! Look where I am. Here the numbers approach 90%. I mean, if these numbers keep up, this city will become the size of modern day Galveston, Tx thanks to the natural biological fact that male ass fucking cannot possibly create new life.

"But hey, why have kids? They're nothing but trouble. All cultured adults hate kids. I gotta pursue my arts, music or literature at all costs. Who wants to have a little monster tear out of a woman's body, driving her batty with pain during the process and wracking her with debilitating depression after the birth. Keep it real to the end, don't let the little ones force you to breast feed in public or be caught with a bald midget screamer clasping your neck like a fucking scorpion trying to finish the job.

"Don't enter the world of inconveniences. Why trouble yourself? So you can think of yourself as God-like because of the one thing human being shares in common with God, the creation of life. But if you think about it, all the human creations are sick, evil animals who can only think one day at a time because the gravity they face with the unpredictable reminder of how family life will develop."

*   *   *   *

1776, the beginning of our country. September 11, 2001, the end of the country. The unpenetrible force got penetrated like a gaping hole in the ozone or some bitch-in-heat dog. Because it somehow seems apparent that Uncle Sam was the man. Straight-forward, missionary position to the world.

But now it was payback time. Terrorist cells turning the Great Satan into a metaphorical prison bitch. The worst part is Mr. Rapist decided to let the Uncle off easy. Because they could have done more. I mean, so many of those motherfuckers were planted over here anyway that Central Command could pressed the red button on the remote and turn on the metal chips placed on the drones' heads to carry out a penetrating and hideous inside assault like a parasite in the human body that suddenly goes bonkers and spreads like wildfire after finding a delicious amino acid and swallowing it whole, therefore giving it the energy to eat through the cell walls and organs, yet sparing the life of the suffering human at the brink of death so that it can keep feeding. Because if Mr. Uncle Sam dies at approximately 300, the parasite also dies because it can only feed on living flesh. For God's sake, it waited this long just to gain this hold just for it to get greedy and lose sight of the long term. Don't count your chickens before they are hatched. Don't be too hasty.

But that is terrorist Central Control's duty. Make sure the multitudes don't get out of line. Keep holding the Uncle's shriveling body in peril but don't let him escape this life. Because he will retool for payback and the payback always overpays the debt. I mean, if one of these toddler entities can stock weapons, so can we. Maybe the greedy parasites can mess up our land, our fun, our wealth and good times but you can't tear down a goliath if you don't have the goods. Maybe a slingshot worked for David but I don't think he actually killed Goliath. If he didn't(I'll have to look it up) then Goliath had to have gotten his strength back to eventually plan revenge but failed.

But U.S. revenge is more aimless because we will shoot first and ask questions later and spray the nuclear bullets throughout the world until we get some questions answered. Therefore, our revenge is guaranteed to work because more targets equal more success.

If some innocents get hurt along the way, then so be it. Stand wooden an unarmed in a battlefield and ignore the "Enter at your own risk" sign to your own peril. It's not my problem, it's not his problem. It's your problem.

You entered in here wanting someone to hold your hand, be a man and accept the consequences.

*   *   *   *

"Say-Town" being a subtle warzone, the casualties pile up like a tetris game then dissipate without evidence that it happened. That's what it feels like anyway. "M. Jones, you should have seen it that day when …" or "M. Jones, Rocky got shot." I missed all the action. Less stress but less action.

I mean, if I have to be a karma cop, let me get my feet wet so I can get a feel for how to take appropriate action when problems strike.

I'll be put on the spot and blindsided ferociously. All of a sudden, it's, "What're you gonna do, baby?" He breaks off a bottle in his hand, looking more fierce than he actually is. My limited training and experience cowers me more, otherwise he'd be a kitten with a claw.

Speaking of kittens, Precious deals her inviting pussy to anyone and everyone. At first I tried to protect her but after awhile I didn't care. Precious decided to infiltrate the group and work her magic and all she caused was harm. I wouldn't call her a double agent necessarily, just young and naïve. Though young and naïve can be dangerous. This flirty young lollipop sucks in the men. I seen it. I saw it at a strip club where she got broke asses to giver her money for lap dances. When a man meets her and realizes she's the easiest lay on earth. But this girl's hard in a different way. She leaves behind a trail of deceit and jealousy with a smile on her face the whole time. She thinks she can have her cake and eat it, too. She can fuck any man she wants and play it touchy-feely with some of the girls. I really got the raw end of the deal.

Out of this entire group, I was the only guy not to fuck her. Not only that, she never once hung out with me without C.M. But she hung out with everyone else without C.M. What's up? I'm one of the top cops in the karma police force. My power is immense. But when it comes down to a red-brown haired Satanic beauty, I melt in the hell fires. I fell for her charming little sweet talk, but now that I have pulled out of fantasy land, I will hold her for spiritual crimes rendered. Of course, first I have to give her the karmic Miranda rights: "You have the right to remain obstinate in your beliefs. You have the right to trump those beliefs whenever necessary. You do understand that by trumping those beliefs, you must face the consequences of such hypocrisy."

She does have beliefs, you know. She attends the local rich church, where they only let you in if you are dressed to the nines, kinda like a New York nightclub where the cover charge is collected during the service. She can't do her stripping here, but she can cover up well. Wearing high class clothes that cost high class money to go talk to the preacher who organizes strikes on rock concerts and football games.

I'd imagine he doesn't approve of strippers. But this fact dodges her dense brain so that she doesn't feel the need to guard a secret. Because as far as she is concerned, at this moment she not a stripper. All she is is an attractive single woman waiting in line to shake the hand of the famous worldwide leader of the church.

I can never trust a reverend who has it that good. It's too easy. First of all, you're rich, which at least should fly in the face of all things religious. You don't see people hauling ass to join the priesthood nowadays. I mean, if I'm comped on everything, get free limo rides, and go on gambling adventures, I'd do it. So at least Catholic priests are poor. But they get riches in bunches in young male teenagers showering after football practices in a conglomerate target.

*   *   *   *

But C.M. knows what he's doing. He always knows what he's doing. So I trust him when he says, "I'll take care of it." He used to lose his temper too much and too extremely. Isn't he smoking enough weed? Maybe not, but maybe he'd be even more furious if he didn't smoke out.

C.M. can be wrong at times, though. After all this crap, he's telling me Precious is my friend. So I fought the urge to argue and nodded my head.

He always takes me where I need to go. An endless winter of 60 degrees, keeps me warm all those nights without a girl. They always say they self medicate. I chose to medicate medicate. This is because I am the big brother to everyone. I can't lose control. Also, I shouldn't seize too much control. 2+2 always equals 4 even in this seemingly sick, twisted world. Always look out for number 1 because everyone else is. That's my favorite qualifier word. Because one is ahead of two. If you are not ahead then you're behind.

*   *   *   *

Shystee update. Speedate 2005. Let it ride. He's the gambler who always wins. He shows his poker hand to the rest of the table but stays in the game because he somehow puffs out a whiny, hazy cloud that makes the rest of the table forget what they had just seen.

Oh, how he taunts them. I always saw that sick, evil grin but my mind told me it was somehow innocent. Why, oh why do the women keep getting baited? These are smart, sophisticated women who have now turned to jelly thanks to his begging heart. He drags them into his room one by one and lectures them on his value. Boy, he sure showed them! And they agree. They always agree. Poor Ginger. His lover. She wanted so much to keep believing him and sort of felt satisfied yet also felt a lacking, a seemingly small caveat. "He's sorry ... but, he's crying ... but he has a nice comfortable house ... but, he always gives me food ... but. He tells me he loves me ... but it's always party time ... but. He's got lots of friends ... but. Why do I hate something? Is it him? Is it his friends? It's his lack of attention. I hate his lack of attention towards me. Come on, this is me! Where I came from, I was in demand. Waited on hand and foot until I found someone more exciting. No loyalty on my part. Fuck loyalty! And now I know why. I finally do what I should and this is what happens. This is the last time I even put out for someone who is more of a woman than I am. But then again, if I am so weak, why do I keep coming back? In a sense I want to train him. Train him how to treat a lady. That's what I'll do. Convert him into a gentleman. A gentleman who will lay down his life for me.

"Watch his conversion completely, let him wallow in newfound and perceived power and glory and then yank myself away because if I don't I'll be sucked in by a creature even more boring than before. Because in his present state, he's a jerk but fun for the chase."

I imagine this or some variation would sprint through her head day and night. I watched her think this one night as she smoked in something that would give her no tomorrow. She doesn't want a tomorrow. She wants a perpetual today. If one were per se, to have a perpetual today, the consequences are endless but do not have to be dealt. That is not another way of saying no consequences. It is saying that you may be affecting yourself in ways you do not realize. So that means they are already there. Tomorrow just develops those consequences. If you live in a perpetual today, just hold that roll of film tightly enfisted, so no one knows it exists. Certainly don't run to the one hour photo lab because then you hit tomorrow.

That's why you keep smoking and smoking. If you stay awake, there in no tomorrow. The change in days involves sleeping and waking. So just don't do it. Eventually everyone else staying in the house will. That means when the others enjoy that warm stretch on their tomorrow, you will still enjoy your today. So now for them, it's the twenty-first and for you it's the twentieth. You've entered a time warp. A twilight zone that protects rather than hurts you. You chose it and you get to live it. "Yeah, I get to live in a glass box now, Mr. Shystee. You can spit on it, kick it, sick your nice dog on it, I'm not coming out! There's no tomorrow."

Grow up, girl. There is always a tomorrow, so just face it. Actually, most times it turns out better than you think. Maybe this tomorrow you will have the guts to walk away. Maybe not. But that's okay. There will be many more tomorrows. This could be gangrenous optimism, but some of the shit you're on could cause gangrenous limbs.

*   *   *   *

Then there's the wimp-faggot roommate. Mr. Kiss Ass, Nice Guy in the shadows. He is why some Nice guys finish last. Always laughing, always going with the flow. Standing on his high faux standup comedy stage, analyzing the frivolous joke of life he perceives. "Ha-Ha, let's watch Eddie Murphy. Ha-Ha, let's watch Faces of Death. Ha-Ha, Daisy, sleep in my room and I promise I won't hurt you. Ha-Ha. After all, we went to school Together. Remember those great times we had? All laughs. Everything is laughs. You know the funniest thing? I put a pill in your drink, but it's okay because you won't feel it. You won't feel a thing. When you wake up, we'll talk and laugh like we always did. I always looked up to you,

Daisy, and I always will. Hey, I got a joke for you. There was this girl named Daisy, a girl as beautiful as any flower in a garden. She shyly hid her beauty even as all the other flowers opened up their beauty to the world one by one.

"The bee traveled the garden and pollinated all the flowers except Daisy. He stays midair, unfulfilled by the one he could not touch. Because, my god, it's been five springs and was tired of fucking waiting. But the bee would dare not hover too close. He wanted Daisy to lower her guard down but he needed help. So he spoke to his friend Licker the Slug and Licker suggested that the bee smuggle honey from the hive and shower Daisy with it. She will love the taste and feel of it so much, she will show herself to you. Well, gee, Licker, how can I pay you back? "Easy, just let me have a look, too."

"No problem. Come one, come all. I'm a sharing creature."

"So anyway, he stands over Miss Daisy, high up in the air so that she can barely see him. But he just idles in the air, enticing her with what he's holding but not bearing down on her so she'll be interested. He finally figured it out. He was coming on too strong. Way too strong. It's like dealing with a kid. You hand a kid a yo-yo and he drops it on the ground and walks away.

"Start yo-yoing it or whatever and he grabs at it but can't reach it because you pull it back before it can reach his clutches. So he hungers for it. Becomes a five year old mad man. The lust for something he can't have. Or can he?

"Licker presented this new mentality to the bee."

"Turn that shit around on her," he said. "When you have the right mentality, you can get even the jewel of the garden. But remember our bargain. In return for your paradise, I get a taste."

"So the next thing you know, the bee slowly lowers himself towards Daisy. So she can see a better view of his bounty.

"Oh, Daisy," he hums sweetly. "Oh Daisy. I have a treat for you. Something you can taste that you never have before. Sometimes the breeze blows cool. Sometimes the other bugs gather at your feet, worshipping the site above them. The other bugs sent me to you because I'm the only one who can fly and give you the treat to award you for your grace. When so many of us love you, we want to share your friendship. But you won't open up to us. What are you afraid of? I know you want to smile when I come by. Just take what I have to offer you and you can enjoy it in peace. We will all leave you alone(except Licker, shhh!)

"Daisy then slightly opens up a couple of petals to show a little smile, but just a little one because she is a hard nut to crack. But here goes Mr. Bee again: "Come on, darling. A taste you need to have. Do you want to live your life and then wither and die without tasting it? Come one, one taste. That's all I ask. Then I will leave you alone to savor the flavor.

"Daisy looks up to a bright sun that will never set, at least for today. She knows it. This sun will stick around to watch her happiest moment. All the creatures in the garden are finally giving her her due. The fact is, she wanted to befriend them this whole time. But she was always "better" than them. The pedestal may sound great, but what is the point of staking your flag at the peak of the mountain if you climbed the mountain below. She had been waiting for this day. Waiting for the kind of relationship she could have been waiting for this day. Waiting for the kind of relationship she could have with her desired minions where they would think they're equal. Because as much as she hated that pedestal, the comfort always kept her there. So now the big trifecta. Feel good, feel comfortable, feel the power. But after three days of smothering herself with the syrupy substance, she felt a gathering paralysis. She would glance at the sky and then suddenly stick her gaze on one of the moving clouds. She wanted to jump above a moving cloud but of course could never leave the ground.

Held into ground in one place yet her height gave the bugs something to look up to. The bee felt this but his ability to fly made him think he could get her respect. So he provided the honey and that would clinch it. But all the honey did is make her want the heights of those clouds. She now needed something better, something she never needed before. But she couldn't figure out how to be with those clouds. And she started to realize that the cause was lost. But she still wanted to dream. Because the garden was so fucking boring. She could at least be lost in one of the clouds so she would not have to think about the trash beneath. Periodically, the bee would come by and inquire of her honey inventory.

"She knew how eager the bee was to please her. So she would tilt her head as he hovered near and she would wink with her petals. Mr. Bee would smile wide and leave her enough for a week. Right after he left, she looked back up, back toward the dream. She stopped talking to the underlings all together. Certainly, they no longer served a purpose. She didn't need their approval. The bee gave her that and more. So why bother?

`But the bee had been making plans. And she wasn't aware that nothing is for free. Or maybe she thought her payment to the minions was her friendship. And she never gave any higher payment. "I don't know where I was going with this," said Mr. Nice Guy. "More of a tale than a joke." Daisy told me later on when I was hanging out with her about Nice Guy's strange story, but then she was probably so fucked up that she was imagining the whole thing. But one thing for sure was that She was in that room with him almost twenty four hours a day, sleeping and waking and sleeping and waking again, Daisy feeling caresses and explorations, electric to the touch. She couldn't quite grasp whose room she was in, how she got there, or if she should leave.

I asked because I was curious. "Yeah, she's his fuck buddy. But it ain't anything. They've known each other forever. C.M. seemed to know everything that was going on in that house, though nobody talked about it. I went for short visits and everything seemed cool. A fight almost broke out one time but that is the only real trouble I ever saw.

I understand the debauchery, though, even though I had never been exposed to it to this extent. But it's an easy formula. Everything is life has formulas. If acute drunkenness leads to rambunctious and rambunctious and irresponsible sexual behavior, what do you think happens when you trade liquor for some magic dust that moves down a tube straight to your mouth.

C.M. introduced it to these guys with a warning: "Be careful with this stuff." But they refused to listen. He knew he was dealing with an element that didn't understand consequences. A rich white element in which mommy or daddy always bailed them out. And cover ups. Cover ups. The parents were good at those too. Did these more for their own sake than for their kids. These are vice presidents at banks, lawyers and insurance executives. These are the foundation of a society. And it is nothing new for a child of privilege to fuck up. It's always, "Sweep it under the rug, no one will notice. But the word spreads and everyone knows anyway. You go to your block party, sipping a few cocktails and laughing, talking about how Trevor is taking some time off from Georgetown this year for study abroad trips and relaxation time.

The real story is that the parents had to take the kid out before he failed. I mean, since so many are having trouble, why not band together and form a community outreach? Because that is something rich people do for do for poor people to show that they are, "Looking out for the less fortunate." But how can these wizards who can run companies but not their own lives be "more fortunate." They can't be and they're not. But not one of these people have ever made that humbling step, so it would be a gargantuan leap for the one that does. Because for that guy it would lead to nothing but trouble. Finally, the framers of this city would have a fall guy. A scapegoat. Someone who would always serve as that shield. They would say, "Hey, at least I'm not that guy." The fact is, the guy pointing the finger is probably worse but no one is going to force it out of him. So it's better to keep your mouth shut. Don't take that risk. It is not worth it. There is a time for morals and a time for survival and survival must always come first.

Speaking of survival, one night C.M. brought me to his world to people I had not seen. Now in the past he had introduced me to some of his old neighborhood cronies and of course there is Shystee's aforementioned "crackden of love." This time C.M. put me in the lions den of the "EMME." Though at the time I did not know it. I assumed it was simply a gathering of Mexicans in the Barrio. For awhile, I thought, "Thanks for doing that to me without warning." But he probably thought rightly that I would refuse to go if warned plus he would give me more of that world he promised me. In my ignorant bliss at the time, I felt no fear of the people but later they inquired to C.M. who I was and he vouched for me.

So, apparently, I dodged a bullet. An invisible one. Did this make me stronger? I don't know. It probably does. It's easy to become brave when you know you'll be saved. At least in the long run. Short term is a bitch, though. Mark it up to jealousy. Watching a bigger man stand out. "Look at that show off," they say. And the brave one could respond, saying, "Let's see you do it, then."

"Well, I don't have to." Acting like they're taking the high road. "I'm not a show off." No, they save their showing off for clothing, money and lies about how many women they've slept with. You know, the truly important things.

And then C.M. takes me on those pointless drives around the city. All the four directions and all the way back around. Downtown Saturday nights, Northside, sleepy weekday afternoons.

I could be sitting on the porch, sipping lemonade in the heat when a silver bullet approaches without warning, a chariot to carry me to a fun but unknown destination.

I've always said there's an id in me raring to go but my actual adultness causes me to take a step back. "This is too easy," I think. Strangers don't hand out lollipops to children for charity's sake. But it is not that drastic for C.M. and I. This one's more like the mischievous kid tempting the good kid to skip class so they can have fun and both get in trouble. It's not an equal arrangement, though.

The bad kid loves to stand at the edge of the playground during recess everyday and monitor how the other kids play. Every kid takes on a role. There are the strong minded ones who will lead groups in games those groups are playing. There might be two separate leaders for two separate groups. In these groups there are snitches(or tattle talers), ones devoted to the group leaders and those who go with the flow. The evil scout preys on this last type. One might call this person weak or a loser, but compared to the snitches they are strong. Because when adversity hits the laid back kid, he doesn't go crying to an authority. The laid back kid is also stronger than those adherent to the group, though these types seem stronger. They may be defiant to the bad boy looking for a companion, but they seek solace in their fearless leader, knowing the leader will put the bad boy out to pasture. So how hard is it for these followers? Their strength is only in numbers and their personalities run flat as a Midwest cornfield.

The bad boy learns these things over the course of his days and the day comes when he spots his prey. His prey may or may not be involved in a group activity and he definitely will not be that whiny bitch who will sell you out when things go wrong.

And you love this guy's morals. If he doesn't like what's going on, he takes a hike. Well now he had already violated the group collective, so he can't go back there. And being the good guy, he is willing to give the snitch a chance. Now, the bad boy starts licking his chops as if he's a cartoon wolf who ties the cloth napkin around his neck and holds out a knife and fork in each hand.

The wolf is very perceptive. He understands Mr. Snitch. Mr. Snitch cannot last no matter what. Even if something happens to the snitch that Laid Back did on accident, Snitch will scream. Laid back is a problematic label. So is loner. So is non-comformist. This character of the human map is almost indefinable. He's a man who eludes definition, sometimes on purpose. He doesn't even know if this gives him respect. It can't give him protection. But this is the guy the Wolf wants because this person will give him a loyalty that no other can or will. Because the wolf will show him power. Bring him up to the top of a large hill and show the layout below. "You and me, bro." C.M. has told me this. And little by little it is looking true. And wolves have come close to me in the past. That's how I have learned. But the adultness that causes me to hesitate also keeps me from rash judgments. After all, my blueprint of the human map might not include exotic locales that are hard to reach and hard to see. So as this process moves from days to months, C.M. bringing into a world of excitement and intrigue, all I know is something is going to happen and this is all I know.

*   *   *   *

I'm a man of stalemates. Always have been. I completely leave everyone alone until they decide to fuck with me. And then I use methods to fight back. These methods have differed and improved over time.

I got into many "fake fights" in elementary and middle school. When these kids realized I would not take an upperhand offensive no matter what, they poured salt on the wound. I'm talking girl bullies, lower grade level bullies, so overwhelming from all directions that you don't know where to start much less where to finish. But even back then I had a slight understanding of the future Karmic rewards I would receive, but in concept, not terminology.

I would love to run into that younger bully nowadays. I would root hard that he would greet me with a smug smile and continue the ambush from where he had left off. And I would smile a small smile and then slowly but deliberately slam my cigarette into his temple.

And he would immediately fly backward onto the ground as people scream and run as C.M. and I step up and start booting him in the face. I want broken jaws, broken nose, broken teeth, the already burned forehead, the ass kicking of a lifetime. That boy needed this. And the karma patrol was all to willing to volunteer. I can't let these guys ruin my power, real or perceived.

Because how much power do C.M. and I have at this point? It's hard to tell, because we've built up a good ledger sheet based on good deeds and bravery.

CHAPTER 2

▼

Yet it doesn't seem brave. When we hang out together, I'm not nervous, even on the good side of town. I also don't get nervous in his hood, which is something I can't explain. He deals with similar issues coming from the other perspective. "Why do you let that white boy hang around you all the time," they could say. "Don't you realize he'll make you look like a punk?" He's thinking, these are my homies. It's a credit to C.M. He doesn't live by old school methods anymore. Branching out to new possibilities. Don't get my wrong, he wants to bank it in the future, but now he wants to earn his stripes legitimately.

And I'm his ticket to legitimacy. As I reach down a rung to help him up the ladder, he does his part by scattering any foes who want to topple the ladder from below. Watching each other's backs as we traverse the valley of the shadow of death. As I've said before, Satan is real, he's as real as any tangible object we see before our very eyes. Real, yet how is he not there to us, that is, the majority of the human race?

It's because of the easy way. If you want to live your life always taking the easy road, you inevitably neglect those around you who take more concern. They care, they sacrifice. You don't. If these concerning people covering for your failures don't straighten you out, you will ride it out to your grave or theirs. And these caretakers of your soul, those sacrificing for your happiness, will be rewarded in a realm you don't know. And that's what the devil does. He cloaks you. He "protects" you from problems. It serves as an inherent deal with the devil. You already submitted to him without even knowing it. Those sacrificial lambs in your life who took all your blows may have been well meaning, but a truer form for me, M. Jones, is that controversial slap in the face(metaphorical or physical). A slap that wakes the person up into reality. I do this because I refuse to take blows for those who won't do it for me. And yes, this is the opposite of the Golden Rule, but sometimes my methods unbury greater treasures. It's a philosophical outlook more than a religious one and certainly more practical. Sometimes I tell people off to deaf ears and sometimes to those who then begin to think in an entirely different way.

Sometimes I use this gift to a fault, therefore resulting in possible weaponry against others or myself.

The bottom line is that I'm a white knight and it is my job to travel through this town monitoring behavior as I ponder my next move. I go through the bars and the clubs, even participating to some extent. I tried out some amateur comedy, some karaoke, some strippers' titties. All fine and good. But where does this lead? I honestly don't know if it leads to anywhere. But you have to be where the action is. And for me this is where it is. The nightlife. Are the comedians going to say anything that crosses the line, albeit a blurry, ambiguous one? Do they carry out what they say onstage to real life? Are they actors or sociopaths?

Sometimes I wonder if sanctioned snuff films will ever be made. I don't know if this issue is as cut and dried as everyone thinks. Just think about if these hypothetical futuristic filmmakers had raised a lobby on the government, exploring things such as the profiles of these movies' "heroes." They could be death row inmates, terminally ill patients, even suicidal people who need a little "assistance." Think Reality TV+Consensual Homicide=Art Taken to a Whole New Level. One must always look on the bright side of life. These filmmakers will only kill those who want to be killed. Of course, consequences would inevitably develop when the star or stars of these future masterpieces would back out at the last minute when they realize the import of what is about to happen to them. People tend to overlook import for some reason. It' like they are familiar with the idea or action taken, even talk in great detail about it. But you can't ever really know until you know.

Sweats of trepidation start compounding your body, heavier in the usual and existent where not before. Plus there's that hop sting, that bothersome hot sting. It's there even in winter because your impending death knows no season. Do you start looking for a way out of becoming this true film martyr. You might think, "Well, hell, all I gotta do is tell Director Carmichael that I had a change of plans. He'll understand." No he won't. Don't you think he saw this coming? He envisioned your scary place before you got there. How? Because filmmakers always worry about contingencies. What's going to go wrong when we film? That's part of the philosophy of filmmaking and it prevents disasters in budgets. So you're stuck, Mr. Hero. But don't worry, your family is taken care of, remember? And then you exit this world. That's what you want, right? That's what you signed up for. You can't expect us to opt you out of your contract. So you gotta tough this out. It will hurt a little, but just get past that hurt and you will be okay.

This is partly what a director does. He keeps all the sheep in the fold. The key with something like this is to never put your life in somebody else's hands. You can a little, depending on who the person is and what they can do for you. But don't ever dive into another person's arms leaving your backside uncovered. Maybe this person you seek for help is in a bad or unhelpful mood. And of course there is a darker possibility of foes posing as friends. The good ones get you good. It has happened to me. Somehow they are out in that other world, a world that has a reality just as real as my own, but parallel, always parallel because they never intersect. Emphasis on the worlds. Because this friend of mine does intersect so he can keep a hand in both pies.

Maybe people experience this play in their own lives. A movie-like snuff film. One could argue that lethal tragedies in life are nothing more than a series of snuff films that don't make it to the big screen. It's always there at the top of the 10 o'clock news. You know, some stupid shit off South Zarzamora Street. Two best friends, neighbors for fifteen years. Gun play out of nowhere. Of course, you stop being surprised by this story when others like it have graced your screen for those same fifteen years.

And me being the curious sort, I wonder if this friend shooting friend scenario could have been some great Shakespearean build up. You know, over time tools lended and not returned. Basic inconsiderateness. Wrong moods at wrong times. Maybe a final big betrayal with infidelity involved. Of course this play must also show the good times. The hysterical laughter on the porch. The Sunday grilling with the children running around eager to dive into those fajitas. That all makes for one hell of a story. But that's not what happened. Yes they were good friends, shared great times. But all it took was this one instance where the night grew too late and the friends became too drunk. Those macho cutdowns you always shared somehow crossed the line this time. The sparring gets intense and one finally blurts out without thinking, "Your mother is a whore." Bad comment? Yes. Out of line? Yes. Worth killing or being killed over? No. But you know it makes sense in Say-Town, The Drunk Mexican with a skewed sense of pride. My Shakespeare farce doesn't make sense in this neighborhood. These people aren't playing a metaphorical chess game. One wrong thing, one wrong comment and you're gone. These people aren't going to fuck around with, "How do I get him next time?"

The perception in this area of town is far different than that of the neighborhood with the local zoo and Shakespeare in the park. Being entertained with conflicts that can't reach these citizens and animals like those of Zarzamora being caged up. And, as a warrior, I believe in this. Yet I give my time to C.M., my partner in this gladiatorial crusade. Yet I'm not scared, yet remain concerned.

When you first make friends with someone, you smooth over the rough edges. If both parties, then they both do this. Of course it won't last, but it is a necessary initiation or both will quickly go their separate ways. C.M. drafted me into his army and I accepted. When I first met with him, he presented me with a business proposal that looked enticing. Beautiful computer graphics, beautiful drawings that he had composed; most of all a vision so clear and pure that it was hard for me to be skeptical.

He came to me, someone who appealed to me as a person, who had changed his ways. One of the roughest around from the area of town where friends kill friends. I knew right away that he had to do his damnedest to sell me on this. Haves don't really want the other ones in, though me being a "have" was arguable. Mostly out of work for the past five years, I wasn't sure how much my name affiliation could help.

He gave me positive testimony from others who knew me. I was smart. I was a winner. I would be the one who would help him realize his dreams.

"I will show you a world you have never seen," he would tell me. I could picture him as a Satanic character offering a Jesus character everything they saw from a mountaintop. Or, less dramatically, a front for organized crime.

Of course, I was trying to weed out his message. It's hard for a ruffian so successful in the past would change his stripes so easily. I wanted to believe it could happen, that he found Jesus or some other guided moral path. Losing his daughter was proof. Sounds plausible. At least as a convincing tool to someone like me who appreciates such brave proclamations.

Most people cringe when they hear the word Jesus. So it was convincing. But this guy was no saint. And as I began to enter this world of his, I started to see.

*   *   *   *

Stories of others weren't adding up all the time. One could say, "Well, then, why worry about others?" Because the entire world is nothing but an entangled web and no way for your stretch of string to escape.

But I wanna keep my feelers to a very small area. My brain overloads otherwise. I love coming in contact with those people who just have the dirt on everyone, as if they operated hidden cameras in everyone's households.

And these shit talkers know, just know, that their story is straight. They'll even throw in little factoids as "proofs". And I'm sitting there thinkin' that this must be true and my opinion on the object of scorn changes. "Boy I was wrong, I could think. You hear enough of these in your life and after awhile you realize that it is 50/50 not 0%.

So it becomes a fucking guessing game. And you stop mentioning the news to the affected party. But one thing you start doing is to really look into another person's eyes and search for the real face behind the visible mask. I have met some gorgeous women who, when I talked to them, revealed an ugliness beyond repair. Even if I could have sex with them, I wouldn't because of the intimidation factor. Yes, women can intimidate me. Get too close to them and their soul stink wears off on you. They can even approach sweetly but when they begin speaking, you see the monster leap out of their eyes.

Daisy became this to me. She emerged out of a new social web I became a part of thrown together by circumstances and then clutching at different realities for each other.

December 31, 2004 was the date. All I knew of Daisy was that she was holed up with Mr. Nice Guy in his room at the "crackden of love." What I had failed to realize by this date were actions that began to set the web a bustling.

Precious had begun to sleep around with some of the people who hung out there all the time as well as Shystee himself. Well, Ginger finds out yet is stuck with nowhere else to go. Meanwhile, the meth is flowing and flying and there is an attempted train on Daisy(or successful, depending who you talk to).

Now, where am I when all this is happening? Conveniently not there. I did see some drug use, but if there was humping, it was in closed rooms and only later did C.M. relate the "train" story, which included Precious.

Well, finally New Year's Eve comes around and I am ignorant of most of what is going on. C.M. takes me over to Shystee's, from where we proceed to the rich guys party down the block. The rich guy was gay, something I already knew, so I correctly figured how the crowd would be.

So I float around a little bit, have conversations here and there. As I am doing this, it starts to hit me just how much my life had changed had changed in just the short months I had been hanging out with C.M.

When he and I first started hanging out, people came out of the woodwork to approach me and tell me to "get away from that guy." So after about six or seven of these people spoke to me, some of them family, I was wondering about what I was getting myself into.

But two things stopped me from getting rid of him. One is a personal policy of mine to judge based on my own merit and not somebody else's. Most of my life, I befriended people who the majority of the "others" didn't like. Remember, I was the kid in the playground who could get sucked in by the young criminal mastermind. The problem is, if you abandon your controversial friend, you realize quite soon the betrayal you have enacted. And then, when you monitor this ex-friend's behavior, you don't see the evidence needed for escape. You grow up like this, go to high school like this, and you start seeing the same patterns develop. The young, children's recess changes the characters but not the profiles.

So nothing changes in your M.O. when you get to college. And when you survey the friends you have had in your life, those friends you picked that the "others" don't like come out about 50/50. The same as the know-it-all shit talker scenario. Fifty is better than zero and fifty is worse than 0. Because at least 0 would always give you a straight answer. But through college, you start meeting the kinds of people you never knew back home and the "others" are no longer around to push your buttons. And yes, you lose out on some of these too, but that only serves to help strengthen judgment.

Another reason I didn't listen to people's warnings about C.M. is that none of them, not a single one, gave me any elaboration, as to why I should abandon him. I kept hearing, "You can't trust him," which was never once followed by a reason. Another caveat was the fact that each one of these doomsayers had been friends of his at one time or another.

So there you go. The only thing a man can really do in his life is to take it on the best that he can. Because as life goes on, you take your path like a man and you take it alone. That doesn't mean you're a loner, it means you do what is necessary to control as much as possible, the course of your own life. As you go, you can't rely on anyone else to hold your hand as you do this. Not your mom, not your dad, none of your family, none of your friends, and certainly not any of the "others" who may or may not have the best intentions and come from any category of those that are close to you.

So New Year's 2005 is approaching, and as I mingle around the expansive, museum-like rich guy's house, I notice Precious and Daisy enlocked in a same-sex, heavily-groped tango like dance. They moved down the center of the room, locked as if they were literally tied together and blue and brown eyes bugged out with excess use of something I didn't want to know about.

And what I really didn't want to know is whether or not they would wreck the party. Because I could guess on about 80%. Needless to say, I didn't seek to solve their behavior. They stuck out at this party like a sore thumb, and as I was leaving their sight, the host of the party walked up to them and gently admonished them to "be careful."

Because these girls at this point knew nothing but each other's touch, feeling each other's feel, realizing an essence they now shared which prevented their contact with the outside world. They didn't know that they were in a sparkling, spotless fag palace.

They were like porno stars, with a need to tune out what could only sidetrack their current lust. And this is what I saw, a man warning when he shouldn't have allowed them in his house. And me, a man who could have stepped in but didn't because I needed to find something this night, not babysit two whacked-out chicks. So, because this problem became someone else's, anyone else's, I started my hunt.

The first thing I do is canvas the party by walking around extensively and scouting out women I could talk to. Usually It's good to find no more than two women together. It is, of course, not good to find one woman and man together. Also, it there is a mixture of a couple of women and men in a casual looking group, this is okay. So I go through a couple of trials and errors and not getting anywhere. Then, minutes before midnight, C.M. appears like a phantom camera in hand, looking like a man with a fishing pole with a lure and a guarantee. And he drew me away from my current lake of empty to more active waters, up a magical staircase befitting the fag's palace, to a huge gazebo on the roof, where it looked like the real players played.

Before long, I approached these two very attractive young women. New Year's Eve gives you easy lines, such as, "Okay, ladies, tell me your resolutions. The tall voluptuous girl says she will sell more houses and the more petite one says finish school. Caught on camera as C.M. provides the camera work for my interview. The girls are laughing, drinking, lowing life and I'm loving the possibility of a New Year's hook-up. I had my eye on Marisa, the petite one, and C.M. liked Sandra. And we mingled. And we talkedl And I was smooth. And I was funny.

But where was C.M.? Kind of dancing around the gazebo, meeting people with his camera, even cautious lawyers doing coke.

The girls also made a few trips to the bathroom. And, oh, that eternal question: Why do they have to go together? As a girl told me one time, so that they can talk about the guys. But then, at one point, C.M. disappeared for a long time. Yet, I continued talking do the girls and I knew Marisa was digging me.

Eventually, the girls excused themselves again and time spent without C.M. returning. Finally, when I realized that the girls would not come back, I went searching for C.M. I found him talking to the esteemed host about a glass elephant figurine that Precious had broken while stuck in the embrace with Daisy. (Like I said, not knowing the outside world.) When it became clear that this issue caused C.M.'s disappearance from me and the ladies' and an indirect cock block from Precious, I made a mental note to thank her later (The girls clearly wanted one man apiece, so grew impatient when C.M. left). Therefore I had no anger for C.M.

Certain details spilled out later about why the party went sour. C.M. told me later that Precious was attempting (or succeeding) in fucking one of C.M.'s closest friends from childhood, Esteban, and Esteban didn't initiate it. But it would be hard for any reasonable person to blame him when he is being jumped by a luscious monster with his own libido on high alert. Precious and Esteban may or may not have completely consummated this lust right in the living room of the "crack love house," but did make enough of a display that Shystee bitched to C.M. to solve the problem.

This may serve as the beginning of the end "as it had been known" of the precarious bond between Shystee and C.M. with once again a big thanks to Precious and her destructive deeds.

Pretty soon after this debacle, I ceased hanging out with precious, with such intentions from both sides. In the short few months we had known each other, she tended to act flippantly toward me, yet also very often telling me "I love you." Well, this didn't help the propensity I had for falling in love with girls in the past, nor the fact that Precious was the first girl to ever tell me she loved me. The suddenness of her telling me this was remarkable: probably no more than two weeks after meeting me. And I also realized after a short period of time, that I wasn't her favorite guy in the world. I found out about all the men, and was even at Shystee's the night when all the fun began to end.

With the various cast of characters assembled one night, me for some reason sitting in the exact middle of the main room(where the drugs, music, and television programs happened), Precious suddenly got up and performed a clothed lap dance on Shystee, with Ginger in the next chair.

As she is doing this, Precious looks up at me and tells me she loves me. And me, feeling like an idiot, meekly respond in kind. All the while, Shystee looks sheepish and Ginger and him talk about how fucked up Precious is when she leaves. I was shocked at how understanding Ginger behaved, but I also felt she was letting Shystee off the hook. But what can she do? Precious just jumped on him like his dog Dana might do; it's not like Shystee invited her to his lap. Though later I found out that at a bar later that night, Precious sat with Shystee at a table where they thought Ginger didn't see but she did. And later they disappeared to God knows where.

Can you imagine your lover, in less than the space of a full night, betraying you with such severity? And the swing from a semi-innocent grope to what was probably a bedroom extravaganza?

I heard it was the violator herself who came "clean" to Ginger, but that hardly undid it. And Shystee and Precious did not start a relationship; so for one night of "new pussy" he lost someone much more substantial.

And Ginger was such a sweetheart. You could tell she was the type of person who would not hurt you. The first night I met her, she initiated a hug. I did not encounter that very often in life.

Daisy was another person I wanted to empathize with. But she was as incoherent as Ginger was coherent. Whenever one spoke to Ginger, it had the feel of business acquaintances at a convention. She sounded so mature and matter-of-fact, especially for a 21 year old. This could be the reason Shystee strayed. It was too easy for him with her, and his dick throbbed the moment Precious approached on that fateful night.

But Daisy was much more enigmatic because all I had seen of her was the incoherence. One night she actually came out to the main room and sat in one of the recliners. She then sang a verse of a Red Hot Chili Peppers song, beautifully at that. Yet when she talked, she stammered, paused and mumbled, like a young female version of Ozzy Osbourne. It was taxing to try to talk to her, and I pitied her like I had no other.

What I was seeing was the victimization of these women. Although one could argue that they brought these problems on themselves, one must remember that women are the weaker sex and just because they fall to their male tempters doesn't mean they completely cause their own downfall.

For those in the know, two things draw women in: assets and power. Assets take the form of money and drugs and power is when you are respected and esteemed by your peers. Often if you have one or the other, you can still get laid. Shystee had all the money and drugs he needed, without needing a job to get these things.

C.M. offered drugs. His cool exterior made him more of a woman's mark than Shystee was. Instead, Shystee was whiny and stingy, not attractive qualities in anyone, while C.M. was fun. Every girl I met, seemingly, was in love with C.M.

Precious certainly was, but he didn't want her. And I was glad. She needed to experience more rejection in her life, such as that she was doing to me.

Unrequited love is such a dominant theme in life, yet people prefer not to talk about it. But they love hearing it in songs and there are plenty to choose from. One night, when I was giving Precious a ride home, she and I shared a quiet moment to a recent ballad bespeaking this theme. And we listened, then commented on what a great song it was, without explaining why but both knowing exactly. While she dreamt of a man far away from this car, probably spending his night with another woman, I had to avert my stare from the very object of my love, with half the car trip left to go, feeling like I got the raw end of this deal.

The first time I spoke to a coherent Daisy was when C.M. called me from her apartment and had us talk to each other while she and I both had the flu. She was nice and wished me well, yet her tone sounded even more familiar than that.

This call happened sometime in late January and it was the first time I realized that her actual self could be very different than the distant mumbler of before. Apparently she went to the hospital twice within a couple of weeks to detoxify.

Her drinking was so bad it was starting to kill her, so she switched her vices to coke and weed.

I love drug slang; coke is "white" and weed can take on many names, ones that can indicate form or style. You got shwag, KB or hydro(which is grown on water and might have other properties very different than the other two).KB is the better of the first two kinds and tends to take the form of a compact, budding green flower. I believe a piece of this is called nug. Shwag is usually powdery and a lower quality of weed, but sometimes you can find a good enough that it is inexpensive yet makes you have a real good time." And then there are numerous names indication the specific type you are smoking. Chronic, purple haze, angel hair, and many others I can't possibly remember. Over time, I heard so many different names, I thought they were creating new names on the spot. The three I named stick with me because of their importance; it's hard to forget them. The Chronic, the best of all types, lived up to its name when I smoked it once. And purple haze I knew because Daisy would mention it in conjunction with Jeff, the guy she was "dating."

Now, who knows what dating really means? Should I just assume that they're having sex? Remember, I'm not the type who assumes. Early on when I hung out with her, one thing I knew for sure is that he would hook her up with all the drugs she needed. And then when I met him, I saw the power. On a night when she decided to bring a bunch of men she knew who didn't know each other, there Jeff sat with her, in the middle of the bar, flanked by his cronies, at least five in number. And he grasped her like he owned her and she didn't seem to mind a bit. C.M. was there as well, but he didn't seem to care about this. And I felt surprisingly okay, not totally though. After all, dating does mean dating, and my current status was friend.

Only one man caused a problem, Earl. He kind of dated Daisy for awhile and might have slept with her at some point, but now that he lost her, he entered the bar with a lot of misplaced rage. At one point, he called across the bar to from where he, C.M. and I were sitting and demanded that she introduce her "friend" to us. C.M. and I didn't even care to meet Jeff and at that point I was just chilling with C.M. anyway. Jeff's crew was practically laughing at Earl as Jeff enjoyed his status as king of the bar. Conspicously absent in all this was Nice Guy, the guy who kept her hostage in his room so long so that now it looked as if she emerged from that room a beast untamed.

Look what all these years have produced since childhood and the recess scenario. Here was Jeff the leader with all his followers including Daisy, Earl a semi-snitch because of his whining and isolation, and me as a man who stands apart from the group yet maintains my strengths as I gather a dubious ally.

The fact is, I didn't know about Daisy's and Jeff's sexual activity until she spoke of it with C.M. and her good friend Lynn in the room. From there that night, Daisy pointed out that it was hard to find a friend like me, a statement I didn't exactly take as a compliment. Lynn supplemented Daisy's belief by surmising that I was "one of those faggy friends." This infuriated me, but I couldn't get mad at Lynn because she was only commenting on what appeared to be in front of her.

Daisy was starting to show me a lack of respect I couldn't tolerate. But there were peripheral problems present. Events were happening outside Daisy and I that at least partially contributed to problems between she and I.

It began with "The Showdown at the Crackden of Love." What I heard later was C.M. had a bone to pick with Mr. Nice Guy, over what exactly I never found out. C.M. had a gift of using vagaries to describe almost anything he did for any reason. It could've been over a girl, though he never liked admitting something like that and I had no idea who that girt might be. It could've been a personal respect issue, which makes more sense. Why he happened to pick this one night, a night in late February, God only knows. As far as the girl issue, a more immediate visitor named Candace had told C.M. she liked him and wasn't with The Caveman(as a lot of people called him), as it might have appeared. The Caveman might have found out that Candace started having sex with C.M. and got angry. This alone should not have traveled to Mr. Nice Guy and probably didn't. Plus

C.M. came in on the offensive, no one denies. Trying to get all the details of this mess even much later proved futile. All I knew were how everyone involved with the skirmish as well as those not involved but who knew the participants chose sides in the aftermath. Some were firmly on one side, some were firmly on the other, and many waffled and refused to take a stand, mainly by leaning on what was convenient.

On the night of this incident, Daisy and I were playing pool at a bar. I usually didn't do anything like this, but she wanted to and I wanted to enjoy her company. At one point we got to her house and she got the call about C.M. being attacked and bleeding. We immediately went to the "crackden," where I was ready to vouch for C.M. I was a little surprised at how sure I was about this, but I could feel it just as real as I needed it to feel.

And I marched from the car, letting people know along the way who I was supporting. I told some of the neighbors as well as the people surrounding the front porch. At this point, I heard Shystee's attack: as C.M. and Mr. Nice Guy were fighting, Shystee came up from behind C.M. with a golf club and proceeded to slice away at his scalp, connecting numerous times. C.M. got up anyway as Shystee let up, went across the room, and as he was leaving, said, "You should have killed me." Meanwhile, Candace was in a screaming panic while another of this group, Adam, quietly sat and observed before collecting C.M.'s cap and chain, when C.M. left the house.

When Daisy and I arrived, we went into the house, where Adam was just inside the door as Shystee had to deal with his parents, which included a belligerent father. Adam immediately gave me C.M.'s contraband and I went back outside. Daisy stayed inside the house. One had to wonder what side she was on or if she was taking "the middle path." At this point, I trusted her.

Well, shortly after I sat on the porch outside and spoke to some of the stragglers, out comes Shystee. I told him, "You want this?" indicating the cap. He nodded and I told him, "Well, I'm not giving it to you." So he told me to leave and I responded, "Not without Daisy." A little later she came out herself and we left. Earlier when I stepped in the house, I could clearly see his parents hurriedly moving all of his stuff out of the house. Then I looked over to Shystee's car in the street and saw that the process was already underway. These people had no illusions. They had no idea what elements they were messing with.

It's amazing how fuzzy this picture got. Because after the attack, the two sides retired to their corners. C.M. emerged from the hospital with a limp, so he took advantage and invested in a cane and pimp hat. And with me firmly at his side, and Daisy going where I went and Candace going where he went, joined forces, and I named us "The Cherry Coke Brigade" because Daisy couldn't drink alcohol after nearly being poisoned to death during her incoherent days and Art because of his injury and me because of prescription and Candace nominally part of the team.

We started hanging out almost all the time but not always. One time I met up with Daisy, Lynn and a friend of theirs at a bar and whom should I see but Shystee. He never made eye contact with me, even when I stared him down. Soon I left and Daisy and her two friends called after me to see what the problem was. Daisy claimed she didn't know Shystee would be there and I granted her this. As we talked, I noticed a particular look from all three of them. It was a heavy scrutinizing look, yet also combined wonder and desire. I thought maybe at some point I could get all three of them, but later Daisy cockblocked and degraded me, Lynn lost respect for me, and girl No. 3 I never saw again.

More importantly than this, though, I now had doubts about where Daisy's loyalties lay or if she had any at all. Sometimes the Cherry Coke Brigade hung out with another group of people that was spending its time in Candace and Ginger's apartment. At some point after Shystee's betrayal, Ginger found somewhere to live and Candace joined her.

This apartment began to resemble the "crackden" with the volume of humanity, yet was much more harmonious. I even spent some nights here, as did C.M. and Daisy. A guy named Mazerosky hooked up with Ginger and a curly haired slob tried with Daisy and failed. It was during these times we found out that Candace was pregnant. At one point, I witnessed her call up the person responsible, but in reality it could have been any number of men, C.M. included, though he was right there. You could say her womb had as many different ingredients as a casserole, but with only one ingredient dominationg your taste buds.

One thorny ingredient to this household was Nick, Adam's older brother. Nick was as assertive as Adam meek, as polished as Adam rough and much more difficult to deal with. He was the type of guy you had to earn respect from, he never granted it for free. He might tell you he was the smartest man in the world, something I would think is hard to quantify. He was smart, but not any more than any other smart people I have ever known, and those people, as far as I know, don't go around proclaiming what Nick did.

So as the two sides, as ambiguous as they could be, did have definites, such as C.M.'s family members, including his dad and older brother, and Esteban, the old west side friend whom C.M. had placed in the "crackden" as a mole, someone who could observe the activity of the house while C.M. wasn't there. This was a rather ambitious move by C.M., considering that he was a fish out of water himself over there and getting Esteban to hang out over there so comfortably.

Apparently Esteban didn't step on too many toes, because no one kicked him out. But he did get in a shouting match with Adam, who was slight and small. I had the feeling that Esteban fell under the radar screen, especially concerning Shystee, because of Shystee's many other concerns with many other people.

If a person or a person and his roommates decide to make their home a party house, there will be problems. At some point, some of the people that come and go won't respect your dwelling. They might damage something or take your food, and they will, *they will*, steal your stuff. As stingy as Shystee was and as whiny as he was, these factors must have stressed him out. With fights and shouting matches and tons of people around while he slept or got laid, there's no way he could really police his own house.

So C.M.'s definite backup after the attack included his family, old friends from the 'hood and Precious and I, two people who hadn't known C.M. as long, but made snap decisions to join his side. Precious proved to be a curious sort in this manner. She did have sex with Shystee, but she also had sex with C.M. But her feelings for C.M. still run much deeper and she seemed strong in her conviction to back C.M.

But then, a couple of weeks after the attack, C.M. got word that Precious had sat on Systee's lap at the strip club and this infuriated him. Whether or not she went home with him that night C.M. didn't know, but sitting with him was enough.

And I agreed, because whether or not to sit with him is an easy choice. One would think she could've avoided him if she truly vouched for C.M., so doubt about her remained strong. But walls of females can be broken down rather easily, especially by men versed in manipulation towards women eager for truces to warring sides.

And there were my selfish sexual intentions toward her. Because if she had sex with Shystee, after all this, still leaving me out in the cold, it was obvious still that that I hadn't climbed very far on her future conquest list. During the time that more of her sexual exploits came to light, I started to feel like I might have a good chance, if for no other reason than process of elimination. But I learned, even from a woman as slutty as she was, that partners could be random or repeated, as the mood strikes and not from a proverbial waiting list.

But C.M.'s frustrations with her were justifiably greater than mine. There was a time, before I knew them, that they had been quite close. Later, after I knew them, they argued about it all the time, each perspective drastically different, with the probable correct answer somewhere lodged "in the middle." He said she started screwing all his friends; she said he encouraged her to do so. I figured they were both probably fudging ot some extent. He said she misunderstood becausehe pictured threesomes involving him; she thought they could have a casual relationship with C.M. being the main guy, with additional other men. With these issues between them, it was no surprise that this latest incident with Shystee caused problems.

Then C.M. told me that he had heard that Shystee made some visits to Adam and Nick's house. He felt a betrayal here because those two had told him they were against Shystee, which was exemplified to me when Adam had given me C.M.'s cap and chain. But I started to realize that the "Smartest Man in the World" could have indeed been playing it smart, if dishonest. Shystee almost became like a character, that to me, was larger than life. Here he was, on the run, yet turning up enough to symbolically wave the red cape at C.M.

Shystee should have actually thanked C.M. for his reluctance to send the army after Shystee. Because they were ready to go. Some of them I knew, some I didn't, and with all the second hand information C.M. was getting, he easily could have done something. Even his typical vagaries, I got from C.M. the idea that not going after Systee fell in line with his newly reformed lifestyle. But Shystee couldn't just hang around forever; even he knew eventually certain people would find him and come after him. So after a while, he moved to Florida or Chicago or wherever else he might have been and C.M. let him go. In this instance, C.M. behaved like the anaconda sized garden snake and not a retaliatory rattlesnake.

The Cherry Coke Brigade sailed into April, the month of my birthday. They took me to a club and had strippers entertain me, then we found a subdivision where we could "hotbox" and not be seen. I coughed for thirty minutes straight to the delight of the other three in the car.

But, alas, good things don't last. Pretty soon Candace decided to move to Florida to have her baby with the relative comfort of more immediate family. The night before she left, I had my brother put a goodbye song together for her. But then C.M. told me she was nowhere to be found, thinking she was pursuing a final hookup before leaving.

Once Candace left, the remaining three of us hung out with each other and others. Even though Daisy was dating Jeff, she hung out with me a whole lot more. Somehow, I thought I was getting the raw end of the deal.

As the months passed, though, she started meeting new people(especially men) and started making a habit of inviting all of them over at the same time, mixing and matching people who didn't know each other and weren't particularly friendly. I had to meet most of them. The biggest asshole on the list was Denny, a bodyguard sized neighbor upstairs who at first approached her like a knight in shining armor. She took him in as a confidant and he showed his mettle on the day of C.M.'s birthday in late March before Candace had left and the Cherry Coke Brigade was still intact.

So the "CCB" plus Denny had a good time at a karaoke bar on the north side of town. That is, until one of Shystee's friends came into the bar and approached C.., pleading ignorance about "The Incident." C.M. didn't buy it and refused to shake his hand. Not only did he think this guy was harboring Shystee, he thought the guy might have robbed one of C.M.'s friends. It's a credit to C.M. that he maintained such valor in such a sudden moment.

So this friend of Shystee's left and we were left to ponder. Denny decided to call Shystee's friend on cell phone to work out a phony drug deal which would let Denny inform police to get Shystee and pat busted, if indeed he was still in town. So, apparently Shystee was still in town or making a periodic visit. I couldn't understand why he wanted to hang around. And now he was going to a bar he was certain to have C.M. if not now, at least earlier in the evening.

The bust didn't materialize the way it was supposed to, but the details are foggy to me because of my involvement. I sat in the car, quietly facing the front as Denny spoke to Shystee and pal. I was supposed to serve as an invisible witness to what was going on, meaning the perpetrators were not supposed to know I was there. Hence my paralyzed position. But thanks to the fog on my car, I couldn't see what was going on behind me anyway. Next thing I know, the perpetrators were gone and the only thing I knew is what Denny told me to tell the police.

The police arrived and Denny spoke about what happened in great detail and even started schmoozing with them about his army days and we left feeling that our target would be caught. They never were.

I always wonder about the good or evil of a man's intentions when I first meet him. Is he really this good? Is he really this bad? Is Denny a shining light or a deceptive voice? There he was acting like a hero the very first time he partied with us and after all that trouble he went to, I sensed an ulterior motive.

As I drove him back to the apartment complex, he said he wanted to be "fuck buddies" with Daisy. This didn't surprise me at all; only the short candor did. And then the conversation delved into the classic, "How many girls have you fucked?" which of course he started. I guessed about six and he took a little while to number his conquests since it was so many. He finally said seventy-five, and I was more surprised that he could count that high than if the number was true.

The current object of his lust, unbeknownst to him, only several hours earlier, almost laughed in his face in the bar over how awkward and stupid he appeared.

Denny started to dislike Daisy because things weren't going the way he wanted. He would make rude comments to some of those men she had over and she would tell me how he bullied her when I wasn't around. Sometimes he grappled her in a vice lock and on one coked-up occasion, he repeatedly asked if he could lick her pussy.

Bullying became suspected robbery. One day Daisy came home to an unlocked door and a missing extra key and money missing from her apartment. But she couldn't prove it.

Once time I was using her restroom while he was in the apartment and suddenly she screamed for my help. For some reason it sounded trivial, but I emerged to find him holing her in another vice lock. With complete calm and no fear, I told him to let her loose and he did. On another occasion, he actually went after me. I made some kind of bragging comment and Daisy told me to stop being so arrogant. To which Denny replied, "If you say one more arrogant thing, I'll beat the shit out of you." And I gave him a cold, wordless stare. He didn't tell me anything after that.

It's really hard to know whether his behavior was based on coke or if he was naturally like this. It seemed too ingrained to me.

Daisy started to think I was some kind of human drug shield for her. The first time she asked me to carry out a drug transaction for her, it involved getting money owed from Denny. Not surprisingly, he said he didn't have it and I told her I would never do anything like that for her again. Another time, thinking I could trust C.M. to take $50 to get a $20, he tells me to keep the money and get in the car and I refused. C.M. loved to spread the notion that he now lived cleaner than before. It was at times like this that I doubted it.

Then she tried to get me on the phone to talk about deals to another friend of mine. After a couple of instances of miscommunication, possibly on purpose from Daisy, my friend stopped dealing with her and I told there if there was even a chance, she must call him directly because I refused to be the middleman anymore.

That didn't stop her new ventures into dealing. She was coming across dangerous people who knew she was vulnerable and alone. Once she called me after Nice Guy showed up to collect money from her. I think they let her off with a warning, but she called me for help.

I told her I could get musclemen but she didn't call in the favor for a long while so I forgot about it. At that point, I didn't want to waste those friends' help on her anyway.

I decided I needed more emotional backing to my growing doubts about Daisy. I called her up around June and told her I needed to get out of my house for a while and she let me stay with her. Things were okay until a night when I knew she was going with Jeff. In previous nights, I had slept on her bed while she slept on the fold out couch in the living room. When she left, I decided to sleep on the couch instead and I placed a rosary and some "Buddist beads" I had on the coffee table next to the couch. I was awoken, as expected, in the middle of the night, by Daisy and I went to my "proper place" in the bedroom.

I knew I would have trouble returning to sleep because I have that tendency and I wanted to know something. Why do people watch feature length movies and entire sporting events when they could just get the trailers and highlights instead? Because they have to feel the power of what they are viewing. Nothing can substitute for this type of experience.

I already knew that Daisy and Jeff were sexually active but that knowledge wasn't strong enough for me to get rid of Daisy. I knew they either thought I was asleep or didn't care, and I knew they were as horny as people having sex for the first time.

And soon they started, as I heard a series of guttural moans from Daisy. Between these moans there were pauses, then it resumed. I looked at a clock on the wall and monitored the time of this escapade; it lasted over 2 hours. After this time, I waited a little longer, packed my bag, stole a pack of cigarettes from her room and knocked at the closed door between the bedroom and living room. They had indeed finished and I gathered my rosary and beads. As I headed for the door, Daisy said, "Are you coming back tomorrow," and I said, "Yes," telling her what she wanted to hear and feeling that she had a severe lack of insight.

In my entire life, I had only heard my parents have sex in the next room until this day at Daisy's. It was a bitter pill I knew I had to swallow. I knew as I heard every moan from her, from what I imagined her physical movements were, sexual positions the two engaged in, knowing that as she accepted Jeff's prowess as a man, I felt like the little kid in the next room who was being subjected to something he shouldn't hear. But it was for my own good. Daisy was starting to more roundingly resemble a barbarous rather than refined person. The one who left clues of dirty dishes, an usused computer, and a coffee table drawer that didn't hide the "For Women" porno mags the way it was supposed to.

Yet I saw her act refined on many occasions. She could speak quite articulately and intelligently and sometimes her wardrobe appeared rather conservative. She also had a generous nature. She did favors for people like when she let me stay with her as she was ignorant of my motives. But I could sense her lack of respect towards me because she was trying to coddle me and I couldn't let other people see this.

I finally abandoned her on Labor Day weekend; this occasion felt appropriate less as a vacation from working on this friendship and more like the severing of ties I needed to begin a new phase in my life.

C.M. picked up where Daisy left off. He told me off for forgetting I had invited him to a bar. Things like this happen all the time, but he took it as a grave offense. He conveniently forget that he left me at Nick and Adam's house late at night, saying he'd be back soon and me not knowing if they were home. I walked home through a few seedy neighborhoods, unarmed and alone in an hour and a half march.

He began to take liberties; he must have felt I was weak. We began to have frequent arguments, and he started to display, more often than not, a shortsightedness and pettiness he never showed before. During this period, one night he had me drive his car to his work to pick up a paycheck. I think he had some outstanding tickets. We got in a yelling match and almost fought after I couldn't hear him mumble directions with loud music playing. Then he suddenly lost concern over those tickets when he decided to race home down the highway. Precious was with us the whole trip and was terrified with C.M.'s histrionics. He made her sit up front while I was in the back. I knew this behavior was a complete bluff because I knew there was no way he would let himself get hurt and figured that in all his days of running from the law, he had probably become quite skilled at zooming through the highway like he was a NASCAR driver. And then, to add to the drama, he kept yelling, "My two best friends betrayed me(referring to me and Precious)." Very overdramatic and very silly. I imagined the mind of a five year old in a 25 year old body. Such a combination can be very dangerous, or at least seem to be.

As I balanced hanging out with Daisy and C.M. after Candace left, Precious and I became close. We spent the night together(no sex) up to three times a week. We talked on the phone at least once a day. We came together as C.M. alienated her as well as me from outside. He badgered her, saying he didn't want her around. She kept searching for his soul anyway. She felt she had to comfort him. It seemed like she was trying to save him from a problem she couldn't name.

I stopped talking to him for a week after our latest problem while she worked on each of us to get all three of us back together. We made up.

It's amazing what women can sometimes offer. They often want to bring peace to warring sides and they can accomplish this. One would think that if a woman ran every country in the world, there would be world peace.

Yet they create so much division in other ways. Put women in faraway capital landmarks where they can get together only infrequently to put on political airs. But make them co-exist in daily life and out come the claws and insults, disenginuity towards men and the savage cockblocking behavior that men act out towards them. And the men might also grow a little resentful after the women have been in charge too long. It seemed to be a matter of time before C.M. and I would, in fact, break our truce again.

Through the fall, I was sedentary like a bear. Precious fit me in first between booty calls and then later when she actually got a real boyfriend. When she first got together with this guy, she'd tell us how perfect he was, then I met him and found out how far from perfect he actually was and the fact that he made me look thin. I guess she didn't care about weight after all. Also, I took breaks from C.M. and Precious to hang out with other friends. Sometimes Daisy would call me unsolicited and I would try to dodge her calls. One rare moment during these changing times, Daisy turned up unannounced at C.M.'s house with both me and Precious present, demanding to know why we had cut her off and we all evaded a straight answer.

All the brightness I felt from earlier in the year had faded, and I saw many of those around me as bringers of darkness.

CHAPTER 3

▼

December 31, 2005—C.M. invited me over to his house, telling of a party or something. I arrived and a friend of his whom I had never met before, Shana, was there. It never ceased to amaze me how many friends of his came out of the woodwork. As we went somewhere to eat and he used the restroom, Shana told me she was in love with him. Surprise, Surprise. But I wasn't jealous because I didn't find her very attractive or smart. C.M. came back and soon she massaged him from the backseat as he drove. But then C.M. told her how they can only be friends. He didn't even want to have sex with her. He must have been as underwhelmed with her as I was. She "knowingly" agreed, belying what she had told me earlier.

Something peculiar began happening this night. A detected a sense of urgency about something with C.M. He wasn't relaxed and didn't make light of anything. He was 100% serious. And he exuded an energy I had not seen from him before. He felt like he really wanted to do something this night. We returned to his house and I told him about a party another friend was having, with a very different kind of crowd than his. I was hoping he didn't want to go, but he did. His earlier claim of another party never materialized, a development he didn't bother explaining. So now I was obligated to bring them along. Shana was already nodding off so I was already picturing something bad with her. So we kinda smoked and chilled for awhile to kill time before heading out, C.M. relating to me in a way Ihad never seen. He was talking in vagaries as usual, but at the same time drew a line in the sand, as if saying, "I'm not going to explain to you what I want you to do or be, but you need to make that commitment."

He introduced the idea as something he saw in a dream. "God" talked to him, he said. Told C.M. to take advantage of a chance to "help his business. "I'll tell you in detail later," he said. "But I need you to already start thinking about it now."

Sure enough, he was cornering me. Trying to guilt me into a yes answer without too much detail given to me. And so on he smokes, preaching the valor of true friends, lecturing on how we need to stay together. I don't know why present company magnified this comment. I had just met Shana and nothing recently in my own life suggested any sense of urgency with C.M. It seemed as if this mood was conjured out of this air. He sounded paranoic the more he talked of our team of three, as if we had to band together because all of our other friends, our family, strangers, enemies, animals. That a bond of us three could hold off insurmountable weight, persons and odds, yet was possible with God. Because God was the power behind all good beings. But how good of a person was C.M. anyway. Why would God choose him to run some New World Order.

After hours of my wondering when he would reveal his dream, he finally did so. In the dream, he enters a church, tired and hungry, where a nun pulled him aside and offered him food and a night's rest. And then he dreamt in this dream and God told him he could make money by leaving a donation can in a convenience store and simply return and collect the money.

At this point, I knew God had no part of this ploy. If this money were raised for a charity that would be one thing. Maybe he thought his pockets were simultaneous charities that he always carried with him. The importance of telling me the dream was to explain to me why he needed my help in carrying out his mission: to help collect the money.

Not only was I against the concept of this plan, but my lowly assigned task was simply going to the stores and collecting all the money.

I had joined his journey, his wealth of ideas, his seeming power; but as he was accusing me of doing nothing, he was doing the same. He "threatened" at one point to throw a ring he bought-with money I owed him-away. But then, he calmed down enough so we could go to my friend's party that night. Right when we got there, C.M. and I headed for the back porch and began attacking each other without raising our voices. It was verbally assaultive, accusations flying right and left. Him saying I never came through for him, me telling him that he had lied to me "so many fucking times." With that comment, he stormed back into the house, saying our friendship was over. Fine by me, I thought.

And then I started thinking some more. I was stranded at my friends house because C.M. was my ride. So my friend let me stay overnight and I got absolutely zero sleep. How can one sleep when the dramatic thoughts of an eventful night runs through one's head.

And then all the people who warned me danced in my head, as if saying, "Remember what I said, M.,I told you." Of course, this doesn't have to seem to ghostly, but maybe it should be despite the sap.

Two worlds had been brought together, but now again went their separate was. Our parents never met each other. Maybe that would have been an eventuality. Who were we fooling? We both broke the law of crossing the tracks.

✳   ✳   ✳   ✳

After C.M.'s and my friendship ended, Precious served as a conduit between us. She loved us; she always said so. She can be very serene at times. At times with a voice barely above a whisper. You get the sense that she hurts people, it's either accidental or she sorely regrets it. Both C.M. and I had to understand where she was coming from. We owed that to her. She was stuck in the middle with a problem she didn't create. And I'm pretty sure at first both C.M. and I expected her take a side. At first, I would tell her about the bullshit of what happened and how it still affected me and she told me to look past it and search for the strength to forgive him. But I couldn't do it and I didn't know why she was vouching for him. And just as she was trying to get me to forgive, she was trying to make him forgivable. She told me numerous times in the course of the next few months that C.M. wanted to make peace, wanted to see me. But I wouldn't budge. I had to hold my ground. My thought process was, "If I let this one go, who knows what else he'll do to me."

But give that girl credit, she would not give up on either one of us. I doubt if we were worth the effort. Our feud was so pronounced that at one point I drove to his house to pick up Precious and he came out to get something from his car while I sat out in my car and waited. At one point, he was less than ten feet away, from my car and neither of us looked at each other, though we both saw each other. A back breaking grudge like this doesn't get cured easily. And she sought to cure.

She divided her time almost evenly between the two of us when she was not doing her thing with her new boyfriend. For awhile she would ramble on and on about him and I would admit I was at least a little bit jealous. But, overall, the idea of her actually having a real relationship was so foreign to me that, as far as I was concerned, it was like she was playing the part of an actor in a play. Wondering about this veracity also made me wonder if she was secretly on C.M.'s side.

She did have sex with him and not me, so in that sense it would seem to make her lean that way. But maybe something can be said for love and not lust. If she truly loved both of us, even I had to accept that she could not take any side at all. And I thought of these things the sparser times we would get together and I would hear about the perfection of her new man.

*   *   *   *

What can I say? Events have become cataclysmic. He started visiting Adam and Nick's house all the time because he, of course, could not visit mine and Precious would not let anyone into her apartment because she was embarrassed by it. I never hung out with Nick and Adam without C.M., so I never saw them now. But he would take Precious with him sometimes and she would tell me what would happen. Pretty uneventful really, a lot of shit talk towards Shystee. A lot of huddling up in a new crew that included new and old friends, some living with them, some not, Nick in charge.

So now I gotta deal with this phone call I just got. Nick, calling me, telling me to pick up my drunk friend. "He's not my friend anymore," I say. "Well he is right now, because I'm not taking care of him but he asked for you specifically." I mean, this is minutes ago and I am nervous and frantic.

And I like the name Errol Street, for Errol Flynn. It's like the Wild, Wild, West all over again in San Antonio, Tx. What is C.M. going to do to me? Is he going to pull a gun on me? Is he going to throw up in my car or drunkenly throw up and fire a gun?

I am almost at the house, looking for the ones with the nice, big porch swings. And here I am, turning into the gravel driveway and I am looking up as I put it in park and three guys are coming at me with shotguns. I recognize Mr. Nice Guy and Caveman but not the other guy. I've got no more to say, there is no more to say. If I could say something, I would go in there and tell C.M. I forgive him. I mean, is he a part of this, what the hell is going on? I wish a beautiful song would play on the radio as they yell at me to stay in my car. I can't deal with the radio anyway, 'cause my arms are in the air. How'd I point out these guys, anyway, it's pitch black outside. There is kind of a morbidity in the faces of your executioners. Too bad Shystee couldn't, probably too chicken shit ... Why do they keep yelling, Why don't they shoot me already ... I can't handle this, I'm not ready for this ... Please God, get me outta this. Ooh, I heard the first pop and lights have now grown out of the darkness … and I don't hear anymore.. and where am I going, bathed in light?

End of Book One

BOOK II:

C.M.

CHAPTER 1

▼

And I done told that motherfucker to pay me back, dawg. And he just didn't do it. And I can't go after them anymore; I made a vow for my daughter. And I extend that credit way more than I should. That guy's got kids, so I have to leave him alone for now.

I can't go back to those old ways. They never led to anything good. Now that I know that, I can never go back. I guess I can tell him no more 'till he squares it with me.

It's alright, some of the homies I got around. Respect my shit, and I'm glad to share with them. But I can never get Dr. Jones to get high with me. Sometimes I try to bother him into doing it, but he just won't. Maybe once in a while, he'll take one hit if it's chronic or something like that, but he won't waste time on the other shit. But it's cool, he's staying out of trouble.

And I've been telling him that he's getting better with bitches. Because when I first knew him, he had no game, no game, dawg. But after awhile he started getting much better, and now I think he's got skills. I think Precious helped a little bit, you know, them two being around each other so much. And Dr. Jones is bold, 'cause he will go up to any girl, I mean any girl.

But that's the problem; his standards are way too high. I mean, maybe he has to settle for a chubby chick for now, until he gets better at what he's doing.

When I first met him, I told him I had wanted to help him. I don't know if he knew what I meant. I just meant helping him be creative. 'Cause, you know, I can draw good, he's a writer. And I started my computer business and I wanted him to be my business partner. But first I had to start a friendship with him so that he could get motivated.

One way of getting it going was to tell him about my vision. One day me and some homies were headed to Medina Lake, dawg, and I was sick as a mother-fucker, strung out, no food or drink. So I'm leaning in the car, staring into the sky, and suddenly my 3 year old daughter appears to me, clear as day. My girl-friend and me were having big problems and were going our separate ways. I'm longing for my daughter(and not her mother).

My daughter starts talking to me in my mind like she was an adult. Telling me about what directions I could be taking in my life. It was complex, dawg. She talked forever and ever and ever, yet I can't remember now hardly anything she said. But basically I do remember the important parts. She showed me inside two different rooms. The first room had me by myself, lonely. The second room had a bunch of people around me but they all kept me far away on the other side of the room. Like I was there but also not there. Like they wanted me around but not too close. Just to fit their needs for them. And those motherfuckers owe me. I gave them that house to party in and all those fucking times, they never once said thanks. Not one of them. I brought strippers there all the time, nigga. Drugs, everything.

Then I lose all my cash, turn to friends for help and they kick me to the curb like a fucking bum. And my folks fucked me over. Made me have to live in the street(in my car). I guess I could've moved in with them, but they would proba-bly ask shit out of me. Like I owed them my fucking life.

And I remember when I used to go to Dr. Jones' house when he was still living with his little brother Stan and Stan's friend Phil. That's when I first brought Pre-cious over there and all three of us would sleep together in Jones' bed. Phil would come up to the door in the morning, yelling at us to leave, like he fucking ran the place.

I stayed with Adam and Nick a lot, almost the same shit. After a few days, they would kick me out. And my point is, I knew all those motherfuckers a real long time, except for Dr. Jones. The guy with the smallest reason to keep me around after awhile was the only one that did.

'Cause it didn't take long for things to go wrong with Stan and Phil. I would fucking yell at Phil, with everyone there. His bitchin' morning, noon, and night. I knew shit was goin' on there, but they tried to hide it from me.

And Jones was always with me on that. He was my boy. I couln't offer him anything like I did those two already, yet he treated me right and they didn't, dawg. I guarantee you, Stan had good times. And Jones didn't even remember me, 'cause he had met me at the rave that time at Phil's mom's ranch, when his sister gave him the pill she got from me when he paid her. He even sat in our car with me and my chick and our little girl.

I had to remind him about that. Already, I had known all his brothers and sister except him, even that one brother that hated me. 'Cause he was in college or whatever, dawg, not living in "Say-Town." But even back then, I told my chick and I told his sister, you know, they was best friends, I told them I wanted to help him 'cause I heard that his life wasn't quite right and they're like, telling me to stay away from him, saying there was nothing I could possibly do. And when I told this to Jones, he was offended too, like he was a defenseless fucking baby and I was a mass murderer. Maybe his sister thought I would turn him bad, and maybe my chick thought I was a loser. She used to say that sometimes, after all I provided her. She never fucking thanked me for nothing!

And I told Jones I had been observing him for a couple of years, that I had planned the moment of meeting him again. He didn't ask how I did that, but I think he believed me.

And I didn't waste no time, dawg. I got right to the point. See, he came home from work one afternoon, and I was lounging on a chair in the main room. I was drawing something, I don't remember what. He saw me and acted cool, not like he was surprised or something. And I was coolin' out and started talking to him when he came in. It wasn't a surprise to him, dawg, because we had a long conversaion at their house while a party for Phil's birthday was goin' on on Sept. 11.

What I needed from Dr. Jones was his talent. I knew he could write and I overall needed help to restart a business I tried before but didn't work out.

After that, for a few weeks, we hung out all the time so he could know what I wanted from him. But I wanted us to enjoy our time, too, so I took him places and brought Precious over and we all three slept in his bed. Some nights I went to the front room, so they could have fun. But it wasn't happening and I blamed Jones for this, cause c'mon, she's in your bed and nothing happened? But he always said,"She wouldn't let me." And I told that fool, "You just gotta just take it, nigga, she's right there." He just wasn't aggressive enough. Because there is not reason it couldn't happen.

And he wanted her. After a few monthe, he wrote a letter to her and had me bring her to his parent's house because he abandoned Stan and Phil, he left all his shit and everything there, dawg, I guess it got real bad. Phil was really trying to get rid of us and Jones said it was fucking bullshit, dawg, like he had to ask fucking permission to have his own people over.

Anyway, right, I bring Precious over and he gives her a watch and a long ass fucking poem, nigga, and I know it was good 'cause I know what he can fuckin' do. And it was weird how Precious acted that night. You know, like she appreciated what he did, but he was asking too much. It was 'sposed to be a Christmas thing, but he did it in fucking November. That can definitely scare a bitch off.

But Precious is weird. She's always been weird, from the day I met her. I mean, sometimes she'll say shit like, "C.M., you ain't doin' shit with your life," like she needs to lecture me. Like she needs to tell me what's what. And I'm like, "you're a fucking stripper, what do you know anyway?" And then she jumps on me like an animal, kissing me all over the face, dawg, in front of Jones and anyone else. And I have to fight her off all the time.

That's why he didn't believe me at first, when I told him he should've fucked her. So that's when I told him. About all those guys. She didn't just want me. She fucked my friends and even my brother, dawg. She betrayed me 'cause at first it was just us two. I was her first after her and her husband divorced. But, you know, I introduced her to some of my friends, and before you know it, she's doing them.

And, yes, I told her it would be cool with me if she did right, you know, so everyone could have their fun. But I didn't mean it. I was just testing her, and she failed the test, dirty. She failed the test rowdy. And with my tests, there ain't no make up work. You know what I mean? And I'm talking about we had just gotten together a little while before. We both was going through our own shit when we met, dawg. My relationship with my girl was over and I was scared to start something new. I guess it was similar for her, she got divorced. I mean, I guess I shouldn't have told her it was okay to fuck my friends, but now it don't matter now ways. At least if she goes of with Jones, I don't got to think about it no more.

But that's why she's so fucking weird, dawg. Why is she goin' to turn down a dude that likes her so much, and is now one of my best homies? And if she still likes me so much, why wouldn't she want to do what I tell her?

So she wants me back and I won't let her, dawg. Never . I cannot take that chance. I shouldn't have to. I get enough play from enough hos and I could actually put her on that list. But that's it. She ain't gonna be no higher than no one else. And hopefully one day, she'll get with Jones. 'Cause it's the right thing. Definitely. Maybe get married. I don't know. They look good together. I see it, but she has to change her shit up. Maybe not blow trees so much. I seen what that shit do to her. And white? Are you fucking kidding me, dawg? She can't handle none of that shit.

One time, right, they had the fucking, after party at my house, dirty. At my house! And I'm talking about a real after party, not some friends' barbeque. I'm talking about goin' to the rap show and my homie, "Seventy-Three" was performing and had me bring my camera and I had Jones film when some of the rappers brought me on stage. I knew some others, not just "Seventy-Three" but of course, they all knew him. So, anyways, everything ends up at my house after this, even some of those, Top, Top motherfuckers that I never met. And what I'm saying, nigga, is even here, at my house, all these motherfuckers are here, and it's my dream night, dawg, and what happens but Precious goes over to one of them and whispers in one ear and motions her hand to the backyard.

And I wasn't in the room, but Jones tells about it and we both start laughing 'cause Jones says she goes out there and a long time passes and that dude never even looked at the backyard.

And, see, another homegirl, Rose, was there, too, and she was acting the exact same way. Coming on to guys all across the fucking room, dawg, and nothing, man, nothing. These dudes were big time. They could get crunk with anyone they wanted, so why these girls? And you know what? It was for these bitches own good. They need to know rejection, dawg. Everyone needs to know. 'Cause the way it goes, somewhere, somehow, someone is better than you. And I have a feeling those girls wouldn't act like that if they wasn't so high.

But it's funny havin' Jones and Precious over. It's funny 'cause we talk shit to her but she doesn't care. We're her boys, she always says. We can laugh, we can joke, we can watch TV, or we can get high. I wish I can say it's always fun, but it's not. Jones and I have yelled at each other, I've kicked him out of my house before, but I can honestly say I haven't been right all the time. The crystal had got me at times and it could get really ugly, dawg. And when you're on it, it's not smooth like weed. You take it in and you just wanna take on the world, like Superman. You feel like no one can stop you. So what the fuck do you think happens when you put ten of those people in a room. Like at Shystee's, fucking Shystee's.

And I still don't even knew why things happened the way they did with Nice Guy there at night. All I know is that he had been talking a whole lot of shit to me in the past, and now it was the day to pay. And I don't know why I picked this day, 'cause I coulda picked any day, dirty. So I go over there, and right away he's talking shit, so I says enough of this bullshit. And my memory is foggy, but we was 'sposed to take it outside, but no one wanted to go first. So suddenly punches are thrown and I'm facing the front door. And I don't like saying this, but I pulled out a little knife and started to drive it back to get good leverage and then, "Whack," right on my fucking head, and then more, "Whack". I don't know how many, except I hear screaming and I know it's Candace because I already knew she was the only girl in the living room so that's the only reason I knew it was her. And, you know, we had something goin' on and she had to be scared. I can't say if the shots to my head took a long time or a short time 'cause I couldn't feel time at this point. But I could feel the wetness on top of my head, dawg. Wetness and hard pains. Then a second later, I'm on the other side of the room, far where I could see Shystee holding the golf club and just staring at it, and I smiled a big smile and told him than he shoulda killed me. He knew where I came from. He knew what I could do to him. Or what my homies could do, anyway. And Nice Guy booked. Fuck him anyway.

But then the weakness happened. I stumbled trying to walk and Candace walked me outside and drove me to the hospital. Sometimes I think back to that night and I knew that if me, Shystee and Nice Guy was not on crystal, then none of that shit woulda happened. We all decided we were superman like the drug told us. Shystee thought he was invincible with the club and Nice Guy thought he could say whatever he wanted, dawg. And me, I thought I could beat up the world.

I used to keep my boy, Esteban, over there to watch thins when I wasn't there and he knew how to keep his mouth shut, and I always knew that. Even after him and Adam yelled at each other, things was cool for awhile. Almost like it didn't happen. Some of those other dudes could get crunk with each other, but in that case it didn't mater, 'cause they all knew each other from their rich ass high school. So even then, Esteban was cool there. And he would call me up with, "Yo, dawg. Everyone's high over here. They don't even look at me."

And back then, when I had him do this for me, everyone was actually still cool with me over there. They knew I brought them crystal, but they did treat me different. They never fucking talked to me the same, dawg, as they did to each other. But I really don't give a fuck 'cause I ain't gonna stop being who I am for their sake. And Jones would tell me later about the first time he met Nice Guy, one of the first times I ever brough him there. I think we was watching a comedy show or movie and Nice Guy cracked a fucking joke at me and that I didn't think nothin' of it. And later on with our fight and I also told Jones that me and that dude never got along.

And he was surprised 'cause it looked to him like we got along real well, dawg. A lot of bad blood went into that fight, and maybe a lot of people knew that and maybe a lot of people didn't. And like I already said, maybe I shoulda let it go. It woulda saved a fucking trip to the hospital for me.

Man, I wish I coulda put Nice Guy in the hospital, though. And Shystee too, that motherfucker. That shit didn't even involve him in the first place. And how much fuckin' huevos does it take to hit a man from behind. None. He needs to get butt-raped. Seriously, dawg. That motherfucker had it way too easy.

And then he left like a pussy. Miami, New York, Chicago, wherever he went. And if I was him, I would stay gone. 'Cause I had my people in place. I snap my finger and they go. I'm talkin' my dad, Esteban, and other homies. Old school homies. Like a clan. Go after one member and you go after them all.

But the thing is, I told my dad and my homies to chill. Right when I got out of the hospital, I talked to my dad and explained this to him. 'Cause he was ready and was even wondering what was wrong with me because I weren't sending no one after him. You can call it the "new me" if you want. When I'm cleared up and sober, no crystal, I can honestly say thing are clear in my head.

It'd be so easy to say, you knew, "oh, I'll just stop crystal tomorrow and forever and ever to the end of time."

But I think about this, nigga. One of my boys, Pablo, calls me up. I hadn't talked to him in two months or however long it is and it's been at least two weeks since my last fix. I'm fidgeting and twitching with the fucking phone, you know. I'm about to drop it sitting in my room watching TV and I ain't played my video games in two fucking days 'cause the shakiness in my hands.

It's a fucking slow burn, so it doesn't help when I knew what will stop it an that the homie I'm talking to on the phone will give it to me.

And if he gives me enough, I can go out and get some ho I meet to come back to my crib with me and bone me after I set up the pyrex, know what I'm sayin'? And then there's Rose, who's addicted more than me. She always wants to fuck me anyway, with or without drugs, and that actually turns me off, dawg. Because, to be honest, I stopped being into her a really long time ago. It ain't cause she's white, that's for sure. It's the idea I have of the kind of woman I really want. Not just body parts like big titties or a big round ass. She's gotta be gangsta, you know what I'm saying? But also not ghetto, ghetto, but like she's real without trying. She's so real, she's in your fucking face and you gotta step uup with your best. Someone that would make me work hard every day just to keep her around. And yeah, I hit it with some of these hos but not one of them is enough for me to give my best. And yes, even now and then I'll hit it with Precious, but only if I'm horny and she's already at my house. And Candace and I had our thing, but she got pregnant(with someone else's baby) and left "Say-Town."

To be honest, I would've stopped seeing Candace even if I didn't get attacked, but the attack made it last longer. I needed comfort, and she wanted to be by my side, but there wasn't that much that was special about her. I mean, she had a good body and great big titties, but I for sure know that that shit ain't everything.

*   *   *   *

When I flow in my ride, there ain't nothing like it. I first started doing it only a couple of years ago, but I'm getting better fast, dawg. But, seriously, it kinda sounds like shit, Jones will tell you that. But he still kicks it to my beats in my car, with a big fucking smile on his face.

And, like I said, I ain't no good at it, but I can't quit trying. I always tell my friends, my homies, even my girls, to not be afraid to fail. Not trying in the only failure. I always tell this to Jones, and he laughs or stays quiet, whatever mood he's in. I don't think he's making fun of me, it's more like our styles are funny to each other. Because we always say fucked up shit right off the top of our heads, dirty.

Like Jones will leave funny messages on the phone and I will start explaining, in detail, dawg, about a lot of different things, all complex and shit and then stop out of nowhere because I really just didn't have nothing else.

But I live for those flows in my ride, dawg, with my beats, my music, and then I go "Right here on the west side, Say-Town, we love all the bitches, we love all the hos, but get away, all the fuckin' homos, and yeah, g, this is how we do, west side to east side, all in between, yo, where we live higher than a motherfuckin' kite, dawg, and so yeah, that's what I say, every fuckin' day, till the end of time, what's yours is what's mine and then like, you know what I'm saying," and I stop flowin' and Jones smiles and tells me it needs work or some bullshit, but like I said, it's the only way I'll get better, but Jones is cool 'cause he ain't really judging me like that, not like "Seventy-Three" walking around like he's, "The King of Hip-Hop."

"Yo, my raps is getting' solid, dawg," he says to me. "I'm blowin' up, nigga. Pretty soon, they be sayin' my fuckin' name all over the radio, nigga, knew what I mean? 'Cause, seriously, dawg, no one's goin' to stop me! Not now. 'Cause when I blow up, they ain't no turning back. I worked too hard for this shit already. My beats are so fucking tight, nigga, they cain't be touched. And my shows will be me, not all these other niggas, dawg, I promise you!" And I think, why the fuck is he promising anything anyway, 'cause I don't care what he does anyway and I would never think he would come through on any promise to me.

And I think back to when I met "Seventy-Three" up at the studio, dawg. Back then everything was more chill, it was about the blazin', getting' chicks or enjoy- ing the ones you already had. Yeah, we made music, but the fun was all over. Crunker than a motherfucker. Weed for all. Phil's older bro layin' down beats and "Seventy Three" and the others from back then were ready to rep. Everyone wanted in and the DJ gave them their time.

See, but then some of them niggas started to care only about themselves, dirty. It sounds like I'm only talking ablut "Seventy Three" because some of the others left and ain't never came back. And plus, day by day, "Seventy-Three" is getting worse. You know, he just shows up at my fucking crib, you know, like I said, like a red carpet, and then says shit like, "Man, you're lucky I can still come visit here. I don't know 'bout the future, homie, cause then I'll have too much to do." And this fuckin' pisses me off, 'cause he ain't no better than me. But I know I can't tell him that, not because I'm afraid, but because that is what he wants, dawg. For sure. He wants to see me mad so that he can go tell his other homies how fuckin' jealous I am. And I ain't fucking jealous, either. I just don't like his attitude anymore. And it seems to me that he was starting to show me less respect than he did other people and this I have to answer about. 'Cause there ain't nothing worse than a G goin' down like a punk. Nothin'. I'd rather die. And kill if I have to. I know he started talking shit about me. 'Cause it always come back to you. And another time at this dude's place, with about 15 people around and "Seventy-Three" makes a fucking joke on me and everyone laughs. And I ain't mad at them. I'm mad only at him, you see? The others laughed, but they were what Jones calls, "The Group Mentality." He means no one stands up for you because they don't think the remark's too bad or it ain't worth it. 'Cause it's only one comment, right?

But that's always how these fuckin' things start. You know, you let it go, you let it go and before you know, you the trash of the group. None of them think you worth a shit and they easily forget how things used to be. I've seen this shit before and if you don't turn it around quick, you gonna be down a fucking black hole with no one reaching out a hand for you. The others see someone help you and he joins your nightmare.

Especially in the ghetto, dawg. Especially in the ghetto. I ain't had no respect in school 'till I brought a nina one day. That's right, I brought it out and they all ran like bitches. I didn't load it but I was ready to. My fear left, dawg. And "Seventy Three" ain't gonna bring nothing like that back to my life. 'Cause you can tell most people want someone to fuck with just so they can have something to do so they don't get bored. It's the best entertainment you can have. I know this stuff rung away with my mind sometimes, but fuck it, I'm always prepared.

*   *   *   *

At first, I got along great with Jones. But I knew at sometime they'd be problems.'Cause I know we do things differently and I have my problems with people, even with my homies from way back. Me and Esteban used to fight all the time, dawg. All the time. It felt like to the death. Every fucking time. And with my brother, too. That nigga had to be real fuckin' hard on me 'cause he was older.

Older bro losin'? No fuckin' way. And on our part of town, everyday was an adventure. You know, 'cause some days you just wanna chill, and that ain't never gonna happen over there. It's unrealistic. I always tell Jones that I used to hear gunfire every night like it was chirpin' of the birds. And, you see, his eyes get all wide and shit and he's like, "Man, I woulda been scared shitless all the time. Did you get used to it?" And I'm like, "Fuck no, dawg, it was scary every time." And he's like, "How do you get through life?" and I tell him, "You just do."

But I'll admit that you do get used to it-just a little bit, though. You knoew what I'm saying? 'Cause Satan is all around that shit, dawg. Satan turns your friends into enemies and makes dangerous people look harmless. That's the hood for you. But yet I keep going back there even though I don't live there no more. 'Cause Esteban's over there for one thing, along with some hood rats from back in the day. And a lot of my drug contacts are still over there. And of course it's on the DL, cause I'm 'sposed to be a "changed man" so's I can see my daughter again. And she is everything to me, dawg. I would go a week without eating if I had to do that to make sure she could eat. She could mess up my bed covers on purpose, I don't care. As long as she is not in a dangerous situation under my care. You shoulda seen it, you shoulda seen it, dawg, when she was a little baby and seen her the way she cooed like she was the happiest person on the planet. And she did that all the time. I mean, how in the fuck could she possibly do that with me and her mother fightin' the way we was. I mean all the shouting and the evil everhy that had to be in our house. I didn't stop partying when she was born, like I should have. I was taking care of people's interests other than my daughter because all I saw was dollar signs, dawg. Don't get me wrong. The second she entered the world, everything became for her. But it's not easy to leave those old ways when you know you can live like a king. And you think you can do everything. That's why I became C.M.-Cash Money. Nowadays "Cash Money" sounds kinda dumb, but shorten it to C.M. and it's tight. It's all about image and I knew my image would be gone if I left the life I had for my daughter's sake. And I can't even tell if there was somethin' in my lifestyle that forced things to go bad.

But it definitely didn't help things with me and Rachel. And it's fucking depressing just thinking about it, dawg. I still can't figure out when she decided she would go behind my back and fuck every guy in the city. I swear to God, dawg, she was everywhere. And I got word of the shit, the worst of it coming from emails telling how she was fucking my best friend. My Best Friend, dawg. Can you believe that shet. I can understand the others-actually I can't them either— because I think they were dudes I didn't know, but your best friend? I mean, that's everyone's worst fucking nightmare coming true in my life. I mean, how the fuck do I live whith this? How the fuck do I go on? What happened to me and her? It used to be so great. We were like a team. I told Jones about the time when she and I went out there to San Pedro park, you know, over to the rocky area, and tagged the shit out of It was so beautiful that night and we made love out there for the first time.

I ain't sure when Maggie was conceived, but we had been open to it. For sure. We didn't knew why we wanted a baby, but we made ourselves ready. Know what I mean? Just in case. I'm telling you, when Rachel got pregnant, when she first told me, my heart jumped. And what I mean is, it felt like it moved out of the position it was 'sposed to be in and then moved back. I know this didn't really happen, ha, but, dawg, I really thought it fuckin' moved. I mean, and then right after that, I couldn't breathe right. I don't think I breathed at all for ten seconds. And then right after that, I was dizzy and I wanted to throw up. But I was happy, dawg. Very, very, happy. A new life. And I helped bring it here. There ain't nothing like it. 'Cause it gives you hope in the world again after all those times when you think it is lost. I wish I could say that it was the end of the story, but of course it is not when later on your girl fucks your best friend. With all her cheating, I wondered if she was even sorry. She didn't act like it, except for the best friend, Sawyer. She told me later she went to see him to get comfort during this bad time of all our fighting. Next thing you know, they start drinking and then you know what happens from there. I mean, that's two fucking stabs at the same time, nigga. And Sawyer was worse than Rachel 'cause he coulda told her no an he didn't. If you are someone's best friend, you have to say no even if the girl is begging you. You have to say no! You don't have a choice. And this mother-fucker comes back later asking forgiveness and I didn't, I don't give a fuck if he's drunk or not. And I can definitely see why he did it. This dude was old, like in his fifties, right, and here comes this luscious young girl to go to his house and drink with him. Then she comes onto him, you know, like rubs his thigh for awhile, then they kiss, and-I don't wanna think about anymore than that, I'll throw up if I do. But it doesn't matter. Even if he told me that I would've done the same thing to him, I still won't accept it because I don't think I would and even if I would, I still didn't. And believe me, I was gonna pop this motherfucker. I'd drive by his house later at night, sometimes whith my nine on me, sometimes not, knowing to myself that if I was in a bad enough mood, I'd definitely do it. No doubt. No fucking doubt.

Maybe that's the kinda thing thing that let me ease the trigger up on Shystee. And believe me, it was hard. Moreso 'cause all my peoples was ready to go, dawg. Guns blazing. To hold them back when I knew I could enjoy Systee getting his brains blown out was so hard. And believe me, my boys wouldn't have been caught. And I can't think about EMME 'cause I can't really know what they do or I could get in trouble. So I could say certain people are interested in certain events, so I will leave it at that about Shystee.

*   *   *   *

I really love my car, dawg. It's a little bit older than Jones' but is better 'cause of the leather seats, the speakers and the horsepower. He can't even get up a hill in his when he has people in there-so it's a piece of junk.

That's another thing I tell him about the ladies, you can only get them if you have a nice car. Also if you can fix cars. You gotta be able to fix cars, dawg. And then ge gets mad and tells me it's bullshit. But it ain't bullshit. They wanna see that you can do the dirty work. And I know he don't do any of that. You could look at his fingers and not see no calluses. And he can't do any of it, He cain't build fences like I can. He cain't put the cement in the driveway like I can. But he can write. That gives him somethin', but if he don't get rich off that, then it don't matter. He also got mad when I told him to do something, he can do. Wash his car twice a week. But he don't do it. He's stubborn. He thinks if these bitches are using him, they ain't worth his time. But that's the price you pay. Every woman has a price, dawg. Every woman. And see, some of our problems was 'cause of my car. I had the probation but I wanted to ride in style, so I made Jones drive me on errands or if we was going out to a bar of a strip club. And we did this a lot, usually at leat with someone else in the car, like Precious or Rose or Seventy Three. You know, in style. We all wanted that, even Jones. He was kinda pissed 'cause he knew we all had weed on us mostly smoking it.

And then we had that bigh fucking misunderstanding . So on this one day, you know, I was stressed from work at this nice Italian restaurant and I was a cook there. Anyways, I decided to go there to pick up my check and then just quit there right on the spot. And I still had some of that probation shit active so I had Dr. Jones drive. And everythin' started off chill, up on the highway and shit. So I blasted some of my rap I"d been jammin' to lately, you know, and Jones knew the exit but didn't know exactly where to go. So then we get there and he almost missed the exit after I pointed where to go. And I said it too. But I guess he didn't hear me 'cause of the radio. So how am I 'sposed to know something like that? So, Jones gets mad, says we almost got in a wreck and now I'm pissed 'cause he's talkin' to me like I'm stupid, dawg. You know, maybe I shoulda turned it down a little, but this was not the day to mess around. I had real problems, not Jones with no probation and Precious being so bored that she came on this trip with us. And my real problem this day was not Dr. Jones, it was Precious. I know for sure, for certain, that she was causing all my stress, dawg. All of it. I mean, calling me up late at night when I have work in the morning, hitting up for weed, all the time, dawg, like if it grows in my hair or something. Yelling at me that I gotta do something with my life. So, yeah, I blame her. I have the right to.

So on this night, I have to deal with both these motherfuckers. It's bad enough I gotta face those guys in the restaurant.

So Jones and I yell at each other the whole turn off the highway to the parking lot where the restaurant is. And he told me the music was so loud he couldn't hear my directions, but my hand signals should've explained it good. I thought he was retarded, dawg. Jones says, "You wanna fight?" and I says "Yes" and Precious screams, "Please don't fight! Please don't fight!" And then she reached and grabbed me before I could go over to where Jones was and basically, she was begging me not to do it. She was talking very quietly. "You'll beat his ass, and he won't come around no more. Don't end this friendship 'cause of what happened today."

"If I do that, he'll think I'm a pussy for not taking his challenge."

"Let him think that. You and I know what's really true. 'Cause it's not worth losing your friend."

"Fine. I can let this go. But he ain't driving home."

"Okay. I think after what's happened, he doesn't wanna drive anyway."

So, you know, I left Jones and Precious out in the parking lot where Jones was probably talking shit about me and who knows what Precious was saying? I really don't care.

So, anyways, I go in there, tell em what's what, they give me the check and tell me not to bother working there for two more weeks. So now the whole day is catching up to me, dawg. And all I could really think was, my two greatest enecies are right here with me. My two greatest enemies, dawg.

And I come back and tell them, "All right, we're fuckin' leavin'. And I make Precious sit up front and Dr. Jones sit in back. I made sure to do that 'cause Precious never sits in front when there is other people in the car, I don't care who they are. So I did this for a good reason, you know, 'cause right away I fuckin' zoom out that parking lot. I hit 50 before we went onto the highway and man, Precious was scared, yelling, "Slow down! Slow down!" and I was smiling on the inside. And Jones was fucking quiet, dawg, didn't say one word, so I don't know if he was scared or not, but I was hoping he was. I wanted to give both of them heart attacks, dawg. I knew it would be easier to scare Precious, so that's why I put her up front. So then I go even faster on the access road and even faster on the actual highway, nigga. And I zoomed through everyone like I was in a car race zippin' in and out and between cars. Then I's started yelliln', loud loud, goin', "My two best friends betrayed me! My two best friends betrayed me! How could they do this to me." And I kinda looked at Precious and saw her grab the seat as hard as she could and I knew she was really, really scared even though she didn't say nothin', just lookin' straight ahead. I don't know how lookin' ahead like that's gonna save her life? I guess the only thing worse is keeping your eyes closed, dawg.. Yeah, that's the worst thing, 'cause any second we crash and she ain't ready.

But really there's nothing she can do, grabbin' that seat ain't gonna do shit. It's just a way to make herself feel better. And since I couldn't see Jones in the back seat or hear him say anything, and I know he didn't say anything, I knew I had him in the right place. Because, you know, bein' a man, he could handle this a lot better.

I had my reasons and that bitch deserved it. I blame her for me losing that job and I stick to it. And they didn't really know what happened that night anyways. They thought I was goin' to kill us all and I did everything possible to make them think that. But, really, dawg, there ain't no way I'm goin' to lose my life over this stupid shit. I ain't sayin' they ain't no big deal to this, but ain't nothin' worth losin' my life for. But they didn't know this. All I had to do was yell and drive like a maniac. Man, talk about a fuckin' rush, dawg. And believe me, I knew exactly what I was doin', dawg. Exactly. All those times running from cops or some of these niggas that had come after me on the roads. This was all child's play, bro. It was even like some of the video games I play. What you do is, you start goin' fast on the highway and you always look two cars ahead but also the ones right around you.

So you're watchin' everything, right, and you start planning how you're goin' to go faster than everyone else without hitting anyone. Also, you have to always keep an eye out for cops so you can slow down and they cain't see what you're doing. But, believe me, dawg, on a late night like this, there weren't no traffic hardly and no cops. A perfect night for what I was doing.

Just smiling on the inside, dawg. The whole fuckin' time. I drove so fast that I knocked 10 minutes off the normal time of that trip And so we get there and they two, just real quiet, ain't sayin' shit, get out of my car when we get back to my house. Just turned the other way and got in his car and took off. Didn't look at me or nothin'. I say he's a bitch for doin' that. I expect the girl to be afraid and turn the other way. But not Jones. I could say at that time he showed he wasn't shit. 'Cause before that, I thought he was. I thought he was a man that could bring it, dawg. But it looked different. The bottom line was I did what I had to do and when he got out of my car, he shoulda came and faced me like a man. He coulda at least looked at me. To not even look at me after what I did, to just turn and walk away? If it was the other way around, I'd been up in his fuckin' face, ready to throwdown. Especially after earlier on, when he's calling me out, thinking he's gonna drop me. Now, I'm right there, and he doesn't say shit. I can say for sure, dawg, that they ain't no way he can take me in a fight. Ain't no way. 'Cause I'm quicker than him. And stronger even though he's bigger than me. 'Cause he's down in two punches. Two punches. I' also nail him using my ring. I don't care if that's cheating or not. Get any edge you can.

I can say that during that time things was fucked up between me and him. It really didn't settle down after that. 'Cause after that time, we wasn't really speaking to each other. It was Precious that kept us in touch, dawg. She'd come over and hang with me and then she'd go and take him to the movies. He was broke so she'd pay every time. Good deal for him. But she never let him fuck her. Never. And I didn't need her to tell me that. I just knew, dawg. 'Cause if he hadn't done it by now, he never would.

And she'd be telling me shit like, "I think I wanna fuck Jones." But I knew it was bullshit. That ho is always thinking out loud. I swear to God, nigga, she can never keep anything to herself. But she still fucked me from time to time. When I let her. And that's the key. I kept myself from her and it made her want me more. I do shit like that with all my hos. Make 'em run to me and it always works.

I learned women by now, but I worked on it a long time before I started scoring. It didn't just happen. But I don't just hold back 'cause of that. It was hell with Rachel. At the end of that, I stopped being motivated. I didn't go out there and just snag pussy. There are many fucking nights here by myself and when I have company, most of the time, it's Precious. And it ain't the greatest thing in the world. She wants weed, or she talks, talks, talks, telling me what's wrong with me. Or complain she's bored when I'm playing video games. I don't need her at my house. I think she needs to come over, for whatever reason. Most of the time, I make her give me $20 just to come over and she gives it to me. Fuck it. I don't feel bad taking it. Well, a week after our first problem with the restaurant, I had her go over and get him to take us up to Austin. And he did it, dawg. Of course, after she told him I was sorry. And I really don't think I was sorry. But I showed up at his house the day we left and I smiled at him and somehow I got him to drive. All the way up there, dawg. But this time, he made me turn down my tunes. It was fine with me.

We had to go to take care of some bullshit about my car. But see, the night before is when we left so Precious could get a job up there that night. And before that I made Jones take us over to see Esteban because he had to leave with the army the next day. So when we got to the club in Austin, it was barely enough in time for her to work that night. But she got there and it was fun. 'Cause Jones and I got a nice table in the corner and we chilled and talked. It was great. Like there was never no problems. And two of the strippers came and sat with us and didn't even ask for no money. And the one on Jones' lap was really into him, dawg. I thought she wanted to fuck him right there. And then when we left, we invited them to our motel. They didn't show up and we thought it was 'cause Precious was with us. You know how women are. So then we get my shit the next day, but it wasn't over, it weren't settled.

'Cause my anger was still there. Aimed at Dr. Jones. I had to settle it in my mind. Because all those thoughts floatin' around, nigga. And I had to express it to him. That's just my way. Always has been. The problem is that Jones never saw that from me. Not like all my other homies. They know this. We all had our fights, got it out into the open and settled it after that.

But I honestly didn't know if I could do that with Jones. And something bad inside of me wanted to test him. Blame him for everything and see what he says or do.

One time, I took him over to Nick and Adam's and told him to wait there and I'd be back in half an hour. I came back and he was gone. He walked home through some of those bad 'hoods. He told me he even walked across these three guys and they didn't do shit to him. And he wasn't even mad, dawg. I couldn't believe that. He thought he was in trouble just staying at that house and he probably was. Just one of my tests.

So then about a month passes from our trip to the restaurant and it's me, Precious, and Jones hangin' out at my crib and we're sittin' at my table and that's when I start rippin' into Jones. To make it clear to him that that deal was all his fault. All his fault, nigga. And I honestly didn't know if I believed that. But I thought I could make him feel guilty, because, boy, I really let him know. But I didn't shout. I talked quietly and calmly. You know, 'cause I told him that whole night was his fault. But I think he was shocked at first 'cause I brought it up out of nowhere. And I let him know. If he weren't there, none of them things woulda happened that night. So finally, I quit talking and he just turns to Precious and tells her, "Let's go" 'cause she drove them both here. And then I said, "That's right! Get the fuck out my house!"

So he bolts, but Precious doesn't go with him. She stays there with me, nigga. 'Cause she's tryin' to figure out why I just talked to him like that. And then she's like, "You didn't say anything to me. Didn't I do something?"

And I said, "Yes. You didn't back me up just now."

"'Cause he didn't do nothing," she said.

"Well, then, why don't you take him home then."

"I don't think I should leave right away, 'cause I want you to stop being pissed."

"Then why don't you blow me, bitch."

"Don't talk to me like that. Just let me stay here."

"What about Jones?"

"He can find his own way home."

"Well, if you wanna stay here so bad, you gotta do something for me."

And she's like, "We'll see about it."

Already a lot of time went by, and we didn't know if Jones left or not. So we chilled for awhile, watched some TV, and awhile later she gave me a blow job and stayed the night. I think she told me later on that Jones walked home after waiting a long time, nigga, like a half hour. But that don't mean shit to me 'cause I had to lay down the law. And things, they just got worse.

I wasn't just havin' trouble with Jones and Precious, but Seventy Three was pissin' me off and Daisy. Mostly it was her and Jones hangin' out, but she would call me for weed and shit. But she was crazy, dawg. Real fuckin' crazy. One night I slept over there and suddenly I wake up a little bit and she had snuggled up on me and put my arm around her. And I swear to God, dawg, I coulda done somethin' with her that night. But I didn't want to. 'Cause then she' expect more shit from me that I didn't want to give her. The only reason I even talked to her was 'cause I wanted her friend, Lynn. I hardly ever wanted a girl that bad.

She had everything I was looking for. Beautiful hair, made up real nice, a sweet, sweet girl. The problem was she had a guy named Red payin' her bills. She talked about him like he weren't shit, but then I'd be takin' her home, right, and she'd be like, "Drop me off here," and it was like five blocks from her house. She had to hide from Red about being with someone else so he's still give her money. I mean, he'd be waiting at her house every ficking time, dawg. Every fickin' time. And for awhile there, she'd say, "Naw, I don't do anything with him." But I knew after awhile she would. 'Cause everyone has their price, nigga. Everyone. And it was such a goddam shame, 'cause if I had to lose her to another guy, I want it to be fair. But all those fuckin' times, her tellin' he she don't do nothin' with him. And me and her were hangin' out more and more.

And also Dr. Jones would call her up on the phone when he and I was cool with each other and also when we had a problem with each other. At one point Daisy told me that Red took Lynn to Las Vegas and she let him suck her titties. I believed it and I was stupid, I thought I had a chance with her, even after that. She coulda been the one, dawg. I mean, I thought about her a lot. I really thought she was good enough to be the one for me. I definitely woulda given up hos like Rose and Precious, who I didn't want in the first place. I wouldn't even hang out with these bitches no more if I coulda had Lynn.

I mean, this girl was real. Jones and me talked about all the time. All the time, dawg. She was fun. Way different than Daisy. The problem with Dausy was you knew she had somehin' to hide. It was bad enough that her liver was damaged at 25 years old. How can anyone drink that much That didn't stop her on other things. She smoked cigarettes and weed and she did coke. Jones figured she snorted eight lines a day. Her apartment was always trashed and you had a feeling she was doing something behind your back. I couldn't prove it, it was just a feeling. I wondered how her and Lynn were friends. But then Lynn stopped calling us. Daisy didn't really know but figured that she finally fucked Red. Like I said, everyone can be bought. I guess he got Lynn on layaway. I knew it was over. I didn't have a fuckin' chance now. So as usual, I had to find the girl of my dreams somewhere else.

I always had this one bartender in my mind. She was gorgeous and classy. But she looked a lot like Rachel, so I don't know if that's the real reason I liked this girl. The worst part is, I coulda had her one time, for sure. 'Cause I was at that bar and we talked for a long time and all I had to do was ask. And I didn't. 'Cause while we talked, I didn't care. I didn't feel attracted to her. Like it felt too easy or somethin'. So I never knew what made me fuckin' do that. And you know how it goes. Before I know it, she got engaged. Like usual, move on to the next one.

And, I mean, I hate to say it, but fucking Precious is like eatin' bread for dinner, it's just not a tasty meal, dawg. It just gets me by. I mean, I'm just not into her I never will be. And she knows it and keeps comin' back for more. Because all that's in her mind is that sex, nigga. She really doesn't care how good it is. I know she's done a lot of dudes. So I'll never fuckin' figure out why she won't do Jones. She just won't do him, no matter what. I mean, she fucked Shystee, who knows why? I don't think he even had anything to offer her. Or maybe he did. But it really bothered Jones 'cause he thought Shystee was a pussy. And he was a pussy. The problem with Jones is that he was showing Precious too much respect. Way too much. A girl sees that and she automatically makes that guy her friend. 'Cause no other guy will do that for her. So she knows she has to hold on to that guy. And she knows for sure she will never have sex with him 'cause she thinks if she does, he'll treat her like shit or not hang out like the other guys. I don't think it's Jones' fault, dawg. I mean, he's bein' himself, just tryin' to treat her right. But he's paying for it. And I swear to God, by now, really after everyone at Shystee's house, she fucked almost everyone in there. But honestly, I don't know if Jones missed that much. Maybe he would've ditched her if they fucked and she probably thought he just liked being her friend. Fuckin' hos, I swear to God, fuckin' hos. When they do these things, they think guys like it.

Or makin' guys wait. C'mon, nigga. Why these bitches gotta make guys wait? Just do it! I mean, the world could end anytime. The earth could crash into the sun. Sounds like bullshit. But I've watched the Discovery Channel. An asteroid could hit us out of nowhere and fuck up at least half the earth and killed these women and women who didn't have a chance to fuck.

And then Daisy comes along and does the same thing to him. 'Cause I know he liked her from the beginning. And he thought she should like him back, not as a friend. And people around them thought somethin' was goin' on. I know Lynn did. And maybe Daisy did at first. But I thought Jones fucked up again and became a friend. But things was different this times because Jones said he didn't wanna hang around a long time. I mean, early on, dawg, he was tryin' to get out. 'Cause he didn't need two of these friends. And it didn't matter anyway 'cause Daisy was already dating Jeff. But early on Jeff and her wasn't serious and I thought that could give Jones a chance to hook up with her, but she saw that weakness. I know she did. And she turned it into friends like that. One girl I would never trust is Daisy, and that's one reason why. I know how bitches are, so that shit didn't work on me. But Jones had to be the good guy again, so now he was fucked.

And it got worse when she started telling him, "I love you." He ate that up, dawg. She would even tell it to me. But I didn't fuckin' care. I never told her back. And people could see this going on and wondering why they wasn't havin' sex. One time at Lynn's it was Lynn, me, Daisy and Jones and Lynn called him a "faggy friend." I knew then that Jones really wanted that bitch outta his sight.

And I call Daisy a bitch 'cause it's really fuckin' true. I was just hoping that Jones could really understand what I did about her, 'cause he was mad but not mad enough

He let shit go with Daisy. But he hanged out with her all the time. She didn't even hang out with Jeff as much. It's like, Jones was spending all his time listening to her bullshit and and the little bit of time he wasn't around, Jef would show up, fuck her, and leave.

Then that one night happened when Jones was stayin' over at her place and got woken up to her and Jeff fuckin'. Damn, he was so pissed off, dawg. He told me that he waited till they finished, then left. And he didn't talk to her for like four days. I'm surprised he ever talked to her again. But he did. I could kinda understand what he was goin' through, nigga. You can't get rid of someone like it ain't no thing. Look at Precious, I kept lettin' her hang around.

And it was kinda funny after this happened we were at Daisy's place with Lynn and Dr. Jones there and Lynn said, "I can't believe you fucked Jeff with Jones in the next room. And Daisy would try to make it seem like it weren't that bad. She said, "It was only foreplay." I mean, why does that matter anyways? And Jones didn't say shit, but when we left, he told me that foreplay didn't sound like, "Uh, Uh, Uh." And we all laughed, even Jones laughed. But he's right, I'm sure he knows what real life sex sounds like. And also, they just came home from bein' out all night, drunk and high as shit, she had already been seeing him awhile, what she gonna say, "Sorry, Jeff, we can't have sex tonight?" That don't make no sense, dawg.

So I know for a fact, dawg, that she talked to Jones like he was stupid. One thing about Jones is that he ain't stupid, not at all, dawg. And she weren't foolin' him with any of her bullshit. But also, he was still trying to get with her. Sometimes Jones has too much pride and keeps goin' after the wrong women. 'Cause he wrote her a couple of letters, like kinda like love letters, and she thought they was great, but it didn't get him nowhere. She still just wanted him as a friend.

I think Jones knew this would happen, but he did it for one last try. So when he saw this didn't work, I think he started getting ready to ditch her. 'Cause he had to, dawg. You can't have two chick friends that don't hang out together. That means all his time he spent with one of those two. And they're fucking guys and he ain't getting' no girls.

And Daisy was worse than Precious, 'cause Jones told me that sometimes Daisy would cock block him. I knew for sure it happened one time. It was on Precious' birthday and I took her to a bar that we knew Daisy and Jones were at.

So we get there, right, and Jones, Daisy and this ugly, older chick was playin' pool. Well right away, Precious goes over to Jones and is huggin' up on him and the ugly chick takes off after a few minutes. Later on he told me and Precious how thankful he was for getting' him away from that other bitch. 'Cause right when she saw Jones she wanted to hook up with him. And I mean she was ugly, dawg. And the worst part about it for Jones in that Daisy was tryin' to set them up. An both me and Jones agreed that it was the same thing a a cockblock 'cause if Jones had dated that bitch, it would make him look bad and Daisy much better. This wasn't the only time she fucked with him, dawg. One time he told her he was goin' to a strip club and she got pissed and tried to make him not to go. That's fucking bullshit when you're not dating him, nigga.

So anyways, I kept hookin' up with some of my hos until I could find somethin' better. And then the crystal came back into my life, dawg. Every time I thought I got rid of it, some bitch or some homie would bring it back.

Homegirls like Rose and homies like Seventy Three would just bring it to my crib. And I never asked for that shit. But right when I saw it, I wanted it again. I wanted the crystal more than I wanted to fuck Rose. And we would both lay there wasted and not say nothing. Don't get me wrong, Rose is a good looking chick. But I just ain't know if she's all there. Some of these dudes knew if they got her fucked up enough, they could bang her anyway they wanted. So I ain't stupid enough to be her boyfriend. I mean, they was gang bangin' her and shit, dawg.

Not only that, but I gave her one of my drawings to get framed, like with a real nice frame. And this was my best picture ever, dawg. So before this, she's fuckin' callin' me every day, nigga, to where I didn't wanna talk to her no more. Then after I gave her the picture, I ain't hear from her in two weeks. So I start callin' her up and a couple times, she's like "I'll bring it tomorrow, but she wasn't bringing it. And I didn't know what to think. Was she trying to keep my nice picture or was she getting' fucked up all the time, not caring, leaving it layin' around or forgetting where it was? I don't know. So finally, finally, like a month later, she just comes to my house with the picture in its frame and I was relieved, nigga.

So Jones and I is getting over our problems and we're cool with each other, but now I didn't have no job, and I had to sell after I promised myself I wouldn't, and I had to pawn my camera all the time, so since Jones don't do drugs, things was cool with him, but all my other homies did them. And some were homies

Jones didn't know, some were homies Precious didn't know. I know people everywhere, and it's hard to say no, especially to crystal. I can turn down weed much easier than crystal. I remember one night, sittin' there watchin' TV after inhaling an all I could think of was climbin' on my roof and jumpin' off 'cause I knew for sure I could fly. For real, nigga. And I remember the only thing that stopped me was I couldn't find the keys to my back door. Can you believe that shit? And when I woke up the next day, I found them on the ground next to the chair. This ain't the only time crystal was dangerous. But after this, I started thinkin' more about quittin' forever.

And then it's getting' to Christmas, right, and Jones owed me some money, so I had him help me get somethin' at North Star, mainly there 'cause of all the fine hos. And we could hardly walk straight with all them bitches everywhere.

And we went up to all them little stands where they sold whatever, it didn't matter. And we came on to all the bitches at those little stands. And they'd play along, nigga. Maybe rub your arm with some cologne. And Jones threw out some tight jokes. And them girls loved to laugh at them jokes. They thought they was selling us something. But we was looking for a guy's necklace or ring for me so we was goin' to buy something from those little stands anyways. But why not have fun? And Jones and I walked along, talking about how great women are. Because they are great, dawg. And I know I have bad feeling about a lot of 'em I know, but really, dawg, they ain't nothing like women. When they cute, they sweet, they put on the makeup and shit, they ain't nothing like it!

It's times like this that I think back to Rachel and remember that it wasn't all bad times. I mean, she was my first love, I cain't forget that just 'cause of what happened later. 'Cause for so long it was special. And, I mean, she's the mother of my kid. Us two will always be connected by our kid, always.

So many times, me and Rachel would just laugh together. I mean, we wanted to do the same things. And when we had sex, it was like the greatest thing ever. I had girls before and after Rachel, but nothin' like her. And her spirit was my spirit. I mean, how can somethin' that great come to an end? It was 'sposed to be forever, dawg.

So when me and Jones went to the mall that day, I ended up getting a ring with a yellow tiger's eye. It looked tight and something I could use in a fight, a real big ring.

I had normal Christmas with my family, real chill. But Christmas ain't a time for things to stop. I still had to keep in touch with people, dawg. I did Crystal twice in two weeks, and I went through that okay. Still smoking weed and cigarettes every day. Seventy Three told me what was goin' down like he always was, acting like he was in some shit.

And then, two days before New Years, this chick named Shana from back in the 'hood, came by with all this crystal, dawg. And sh wanted me but I ain't wanted her just the shit she brought with her. And there we was, for two straight days, nigga, getting high and comin' down. And I never touched her. I never once wanted to touch her in that whole two days, dawg. Crystal don't do me like that. It don't make me wanna fuck. But again I felt on top of the world. For them two days, they was no problems and I hardly ever talked to Shana. I don't even think my parents showed up, and if they did, I ain't notice. And I saw some crazy shit in my mind and then I had the dream that coulda changed my life forever.

So around this time, I had a dream that could help my company I wanted to start for a long, long time now. And Jones was helping me with it, but he weren't doing enough. So he told me he knew about a party for New Year's and I called him to my house so I could tell him about my idea. My idea was from a dream.

In my dream, I end up at a church for some reason('cause I ain't never go to church) and a nun there takes me to a back room so I could sleep there and have some food. So I go to sleep there and God comes to me in a dream and gives me a plan to make the money I need" Put donation cans in convenience store and collect all that money we would need. All I would ask is for Dr. Jones to help me.

So I tell him this and he gets fuckin' pissed, dawg! Telling me how my plan was dishonest and he won't do it. He didn't believe that God told me to do it. He said, I don't know where you heard that from, but it wasn't God." And he said you do that for some saint, I ain't remember who and they ain't no way he would help me do this. And then I got pissed. 'Cause he thought I was full of shit and I really didn't think I was.

Then I told him I would chunk that ring he gave me out in the street and he just said, "You can't make me do this." And then it was fuckin' weird 'cause our argument stopped and a little while later, we chose to go to a party at his friends' house. This whole time Shana is quiet and don't say nothin' till we go to Sonic for a coupla sodas and she massaged me from the backseat and I had to tell her I don't see her that way. I hate to do that 'cause it lets the girl down, but I have to or she thinks she has a chance. Now, I did mess around with her in the past, but it was the past and on that night, I felt nothin' for her, dawg. But I knew for sure I coulda fucked someone that night. I had options.

So anyways, we go to Jones' friend's party in my car. Most of time I say my car 'cause it looks tight, not like his. And Shana's in the back seat, already fallin' asleep. And Jones hoped it was a big crowd so no one would notice her. I think he didn't like her moon boots. They was in style but they looked bad to him.

And this dude's house was way on the North Side, but that ain't bother me, long as I'm driving. And, man, did we keep our mouths shut. This weren't no fun at all. But I wanted to get out my house, and maybe our moods coulda changed at the party. I know that's what he wanted.

And I already met his friend and the guy's wife. They seemed cool to me. So we go in there, right, and the first thing you see is Shana grabbin' a chair and snoozin'. I just happened to look at Jones lookin' at her and he looked worried, dawg. I know he weren't happy with me, but fuck him, you know what I mean? This was his problem, not mine, so I didn't care how this turned out for him. So we talked to some people then we went to the back porch and sat down and started talking more.

This talk was worse than the one at home, but we was a lot quieter. And believe me, I was still mad that he said no to my idea. And I told him how he did nothin' for me. Nothin' for me. And then he's like, "What about all the interviews I got you." And I told him it didn't mean shit. And I don't even know if that's true. I just wanted to make him feel like I did that day. I can admit it, dawg, I wanted to bring the whole world down with me that day. So maybe he did things for me in the past. But that was the past, nigga. Now was all that counted and the latest thing I wanted was what he said no to. And how could I count on him in the future? I didn't know. So then after that, he told me tat I lied to him so many times and I told him it was bullshit. 'Cause it was. So I got up from the chair and I walked into the house and told him, "You're not my friend anymore." I went inside, woke up Shana from the chair and told them I was taking her home and coming back. And I never went back to that party, dawg.

I left that house. I took Shana home and I went home and crashed out. And then like at 2:30 in the morning, fucking Precious call to bitch me out about what I did to Jones. What I did to Jones? But I didn't want to talk to that ho, so I said, "Shut up, bitch!" and hanged up. So I know for sure that Jones called her that night and she took his side. I didn't strap this time like with Nice Guy, but I knew they was goin' to be a time for Jones to get his, and I thought about all the different ways when I tried to go back to sleep that night.

CHAPTER 2

▼

So then I had to think about a coupla things in my life without Jones. I needed a partner for my business and I hanged out with him all the time. I mean, in the past, him and Precious came over and most of the time make fun of her. It was our thing, nigga.

And then other times, she'd come over by herself and we'd fuck. And at first, she weren't giving me none and thought she were sticking up for Jones. But after awhile, we was hittin' it again like before. And you gotta see her in bed, dawg. She's like an animal. And then she always says that I come too quick. Like how long I 'sposed to last anyways, dawg? As long as I get off, that's all that matters. And she bitches about it every time, dawg. But then she keeps comin' back anyways, so why should I change. And when me and Jones stopped bein' friends, I knew for sure she weren't fuckin' him. I just knew. She never even talked about him. Not at first. But also, this is when she started seeing Miller. And that was really fucked up. 'Cause she knew this dude for awhile, you know, meeting him at the club 'cause he was the restroom attendant. And she brought him up every once in a while, and sayin' shit like they ain't no way she would do this guy. Never be more than a friend. Jones would hear some this shit and shake his head 'cause he didn't believe her and he thought he was way better lookin' than Miller, which I think he was,too. So when we started knowing that she was with Miller, Jones never wanted to talk about it, especially when he had to deal with her telling him that if he lost weight, she would fuck him for sure. One time she even said that in front of Rose and Rose called her shallow. 'Cause Miller was fatter than Jones and she said she liked "her baby" just the way he was. I would think that by this time that this was happening, Jones finally gave up hope of ever hittin' it with Precious. And it sucks, 'cause he always wanted her, you know, at least one fuck. But one time, Jones told me he was in love with her, and it might be true.

Anyway, when she started showing up less, I just got together more with my other hos and bang new ones I met.

I spent a lot more time goin' to bars and homies' parties and I hooked up. So I didn't need Precious. And I still made her give me flow every time she came to my crib. Every single time. And not to bring Miller. And she knew she had to do that every single time. And she kept coming back anyways. I owned her, even now that she had Miller. She brought up Jones a coupla times, saying she asked him to come over to my crib and he said no. But she ain't got my permission and that ain't cool.

I ain't sayin' I wouldn't let him in, but also I weren't ready to see him. And when she talked about him, I looked at her fuckin' mean, dawg, and she'd shut the fuck up. So now, not Jones around, I started hanging out a lot at Nick and Adam's house. And it was strange over there.

First of all, Nick and Adam lived there with they parents. Then with everyone leaving Shystee's house, some of them had to find somewheres to go, like Ginger, Shystee's ex who Shystee cheated with Precious on. And Ginger hooked up with Mazeroski when all the drama popped. And they got together quick, dawg, right after the attack. So after a long time, I don't know how long, they move in with the brothers and I thought I saw some other dude there, and anyways Nick had to build an extra room on the house and I guess the parents didn't care. So anyways, Mazeroski and Ginger is still al couple when they moved in. But, then, only a little while later, they broke up, and believe me, I saw how things changed. 'Cause at first, everyone was friendly with each other, but when they broke up they couldn't get along, dawg, I even noticed how fucked up and tense it was. And this was when Nick made his move on Ginger. Rowdy, nigga. 'Cause in the past he didn't like her that way or she was with Shystee and then Mazeroski or Ginger didn't like him that way(she called Nick her best friend). So anyways, Nick and Ginger hook up and no one's getting along 'cause of this thing and also Adam got his girlfriend pregnant so he was worried about his own shit and his girl was a bitch too, dirty.

So after I started goin' over there after Jones and I weren't cool no more, things got more chill. But they would all got a job at the same place and then they would quit or get fired and Adam had to stop working anyways 'cause his girl was due soon.

One reason I went over there so much was 'cause I thought they might know where Shystee was. 'Cause I heard things, dawg, and a year later after the attack, I still heard some thing that he might be around, or kept visiting Say-Town. I heard he might've been visiting, Nick or Adam's. I ain't had no way of knowing if that were true. I mean, these people are 'sposed to be homies, but they known him way fuckin' longer than they known me.

And them motherfuckers stick together, dirty. They talk shit about each other behind they backs, then fuckin' smile when they see each other. I gotta say that sometimes I do that too, but I also say shit to dudes' faces and I ain't sayin' they scared, they just hidin' so they can keep an edge. And I know Nick's bad about this. And I think back, I think back to that time about who took my side and who took Shystee's side.

Of course, fuckin' Nice Guy was with Shystee and Esteban had my back, nigga. But then, after that, I ain't really know for sure. I knew Candace had my back 'cause she screamed that night in that room and took me to the hospital and took care of me after that, but she's gone, now, nigga, and that ain't do me no good here.

And Adam was there, too, keepin' his mouth shut, not doin' nothin' to help me, but at least he gave Jones my cap and the head of my chain later. Daisy and Jones got there right after it happened. That's what Jones told me. They was takin' all Shystee's shit out the house when they got there and then Jones and Daisy went in the house and Adam gave Jones my shit, right, and then went to the front porch, where all these people were chilling and talking. But Daisy stayed in the house for a long time while Jones waited outside. She didn't have to do that, and when Jones told me about it, I couldn't trust her, even later all them times hanging out with her.

And what about Precious? She was the worst out of all them niggas. First, she's callin' me up, tellin' me she's gonna get that motherfucker and get a gun and all this bullshit. Then I heard later that Shystee went to see her at her strip club and she sat on his lap all cuddly and shit. And she might've fucked him that night, I don't even know. But I bet she did and she fuckin' denied it, dawg. I don't remember who I heard that from. I heard some people talkin' about it, but I heard what I heard and I believe it. I guess she thought no one would find out. But all <u>Shystee</u> had to do was tell someone like Nick or Nice Guy or some of the dudes that always hung out at that house or Bill, who was one of they room-mates.

The reason I don't know where I heard them things is 'cause they came from different areas. Even people I know that they didn't said shit about the strip club with Precious or he's back in town.

One of the only guys I know for sure who had my back that night was Jones. Jones repped and Candace repped and that was it. In front of everyone, Shystee told him to give him my cap and he didn't. Then he told Shystee to send Daisy out or he wouldn't leave. So he sent her out. He shoulda left that bitch there. I swear to God I fuckin' bet anything he talked to her in that house to see what she could help him with. He coula been tryin' to keep homies in this town so he could still come back and see them. And I can understand this when they fuckin' knew each other they whole fuckin' life, but Precious only knew him after I did, harldy any fuckin' time at all.

That bitch always thinks she can do whatever she wants and that's okay. She's 'sposed to be my friend, so when that ball is rolled, she shoulda jumped to my side. But she didn't. I still hanged out with her after that, but I really shoulda ditched her, dawg. Rowdy. I don't know what it is, but I ain't never got rid of her. And during the time me and Jones stopped being friends, I would think about who got my back that night. And it was Jones. A soldier I could count on. I could tell you it's the crystal or long nights on my own, or bullshit in my mind, but I don't have a reason for what I did on New Year's Eve.

I mean, I wanted him to do what I said and when he said no, it was something I couldn't accept. All I could think was, "Look at him. This guy ain't shit. I'll drop him in two punches. Two punches, dirty."

But he stood up to me and all the sudden I weren't sure I could beat him. So, yeah, it was a fuckin' mistake and I had to go forward.

So I visited Nick and Adam when Jones weren't around no more, and of course Rose gettin' me back on crystal, got job, lost a job, sellin' here and there. Seventy Three was coming by a lot, telling me about all his drama at home where he lived on the east side. One time I told him, "Yo, why don't you move out." And he said, "Ain't no way, nigga. Them's my homies." You know, reppin; and all that bullshit. And of course he wants to be hard. But he ain't that hard. I ain't never been scared of that nigga. He's bigger, but slower. And he comes in my crib, talkin' about he's gonna blow up. He put out a record and it's pretty tight, but he acts like I'm lucky to see him. For real, nigga. Talkin' about he's been on the radio. I ain't never heard him on the radio. He's my boy but I gotta get me respect back from him. Back on the day, he was cool. Didn't have many tunes from our little recording studio, but he got better. I just gotta say, if you're all that, get a better crib, dawg. But during this time, the worst was when me and

Seventy Three head out to a party at a record producer's hose. And there was some rappers and some other hard motherfuckers. So Seventy Three made a comment at me and everyone laughed, nigga, so then I owed him one.

It weren't just Seventy Three and Rose and Precious. I looked yp some old school homies. And when I called them, they was glad to hear from me. So, you know, I saw my West Side guy a couple times, Ace. Ace could get any hos on this planet. So we go to one of them bars, I don't remember, and we took back a girl each that night, and we talked and got down.

A coupla times I hung with John Vato, a rapper. Now that's my boy. I always wanted him to come over all the time and not Seventy Three.

But the way things go with me is a pick a coupla homies and hang out with them so I don't see all my other homies hardly at all. I spent all that time with Jones, and now that he was gone, I needed other people.

But Precious came by all the time. And soon she started talking about Jones, where they hanged out or whatever. And I'd be a little happy to hear it.

One day, she asked me if she could bring Jones to my crib. I said okay. But she came back two days dater saying he wouldn't come and then said is there anything you want me to tell Jones. And I said, "Naw." I wasn't pissed off because he had to be okay with it. I told her she can't make him do it.

*   *   *   *

And why it happened this way I'll never know. I've been to Nick's and Adam's so many times, nigga. So I went in as usual, right, and they got the weed and they told me to sit in the big chair, the recliner. They had some good schwag, so I start rollin' the blunt and looked down to lick the sides … and then real quick I got pushed back in the recliner and dropped everything, the blunt and the weed … I looked up real quick and saw Nick standing over me with a real evil look and I'm about to scream, dawg, and suddenly Mazeroski punches me real hard on the mouth and says, "Shut up. Stay quiet. You don't know who you're fuckin' with." So they put duck tape over my mouth, I don't know who, and Mazeroski punches me again. Then he walked over behind me and I started choking 'cause he had a wire around my neck.

And he was fucking strong, nigga, he was so fuckin' thin. So Nick brings out the phone, but I'm not passing out, they keeping me alive, and I hear Nick say, "Jones, your friend is drunk, he wants you to pick him up." I never wanted to yell so bad. Then, out of nowhere, Shystee walks into the room and stares at me rowdy, dawg. Then he says, "Now you can't do anything, C.M. We got you here and your gone. We'll take care of Jones, too, when he gets here. You shoulda let up. Now I can come here whenever I want. Right when he gets here, you're dead."

So I saw lights come through the window. But I couldn't get loose 'cause Mazeroski had the wire around my neck and Nick and Adam were holding me in place. Where the fuck was Ginger? Who knows what happened to her? Man, I'm sorry, Dr. Jones, I'm sorry. And Precious. I really do love and care about you, too. The three of us was like family, we hung out so much. And then my real family. When I really needed help, you were there. You just wanted me to grow up and take care of myself. And my brother, we was like teammates, dawg. I had your back and you really had mine. My daughter, I'll never see you again. Every day I was without you felt like a year. Now that I feel this and I know there is no hope, I would do anything to go back in time and force myself to stay with your mother or work harder to pay child support. Rachel, I still love you. Because that's what love is. That we support each other no matter what. We both did a bad job of that at the end and we both coulda stepped back, girl, and actually looked at what we was doing. All my friends far in the past. All the pictures of them moving so fast in my mind that I can barely tell who it is till it moves on to someone else. Guys, girls, homies and homegirls. Layin' around with the crystal and laughing with the weed. Those days I was ballin' and they came to my house and I gave them a good time. Now it don't mean shit, now it don't mean nothin'. But after all this, all I can really think about is what went wrong with me and Jones. 'Cause, you know, we coulda got through our problems to fight these worthless motherfuckers. I feel a tear, dawg, and there are those goddamned lights. They gonna get him. Two dudes with guns went out there, I don't know, they're all quiet now so they can shoot Jones when he drives up …

✳   ✳   ✳   ✳

Now all I have to do is sit here. I've been doing this a long while now, sittin' at my stand, drawing the people in my room. One time, dawg, they was like twenty-five people in here and I had all the peace and quiet to draw my pictures. They don't talk to me, dawg, and I ain't need them to. I feel okay. Somehow I feel loved, nigga. Like they lovin' me from far away.

I don't know how long it's been, but my daughter had been in the room twice, once when when she was six, the other when she was ten. She's grown up so much and I'm so proud. I don't hate Rachel anymore. I don't really hate anyone anymore, dawg. What about Shystee? I don't know. Maybe one day I can see him.

I learned since I been here not to hate. I know God gave me this 'cause I really needed it, dawg. I don't eat, I don't sleep, I don't go to the bathroom, I just draw, draw, draw.

The first time I drew Rachel naked in this room I liked it but it weren't no big deal. And no matter what I draw, I add it to a pile. The pile is getting pretty high, nigga. Maybe I can enter my daughter's brain so she'll draw like me. But probably I'll just stay right here.

Sometimes I'm by myself in here. That's when I draw my visions. Some would call it end of the world stuff, others fantasy. There's chambers and dimensions and even here I can draw them. I get do this forever, dawg! And that's all I want to do. I don't wanna get high. I don't want money. I can look at everyone I love from far away and have something to remember from them.

This is it. I will never leave this place. Never, dawg. So just keep on comin' to me.

End of Book Two

BOOK III:

PRECIOUS

CHAPTER 1

▼

I take a lot of long walks. You know, to clear my head and shit. No matter what happens in my life, I take these walks.

Or poetry. I love writing poetry but I never know if I wanna do anything with it. Jones always liked my poems. But no one else seems to care. C.M. always had his drawings but he never said nothing either.

Jones said it was something unique I did. Like no one ever wrote poems the way I did. But I don't even know if that's good or bad. Why can't my poems just be good?

I would say my real career will be in Real Estate. I wanna dress up real nice, act like a lady, and show people nice homes. I think C.M. came into my apartment one day and told me, "How the fuck you gonna be in Real Estate if you can't take care of your own house?"

And he had a point 'cause my place was real messy and it had no furniture. For awhile, I had Jones sleep with me every night at my place, but no sex. He always respected me, dawg. He always treated me right. He knew I wouldn't have sex with him, and most of the time, he didn't make an move.

Of course, there was that one time when me, C.M., and Dr. Jones was sleeping together at my place and suddenly in the night, he kissed me first on the shoulder, then on the back, then reached over and kissed me on the cheek. Then I asked him, "Am I your little girl?" And he said, "I'd like you to be." Then I turned around and acted like I was kissing him and then stopped short. I don't know why I teased him like that, but I kinda did stuff like that to him a lot.

'Cause I knew he liked it. I almost couldn't help it. And I tried to give him hints. I'd tell him that C.M. always attracted me 'cause he always acted like he didn't give a fuck. That always drove me wild. I think sometimes Jones pretended to be that way with me but it didn't fool me. And man, I knew he could get jealous or depressed about it. One time he yelled at me and cussed me out because I told him I fucked someone who Jones thought didn't have a chance with me. And at first that guy didn't, but I started liking him, so fuck it, right? And later on, the guy was named Miller, became my boyfriend.

But the real reason Jones was pissed about this was 'cause Miller was actually fatter than Jones and I always told Jones in the past that if he lost weight, I would fuck him. And now Here I am fucking a guy who's bigger. And I liked Miller's body, I told Jones that and Jones basically said he wasn't good enough no matter what he did. And I always told him it wasn't like that. So he heard about all the guys I fucked and he got jealous. He thought he was better than most of them. And to be honest, I can't explain why I did this. I told him it would ruin our friendship a lot of times and he didn't give a shit about that. He never really liked being my friend, but he still hung out with me. So sometimes I would tell him things so that he would keep staying around. I would lead him on sometimes, telling him shit like, "Maybe one day I'll fall in love with you." Or I'd drop tiny little hints or even just words here and there to make him think we might start a relationship. And it was bullshit 'cause there ain't no way. But I needed a male friend and he was perfect for it.

I also told him one time that he'd be the best boyfriend ever. So then he said, "What's stopping you?" And I didn't have an answer. But I really did love him. I told him all the time and meant it. And I can even say I loved him that way just a little bit. You see, I tell a lot of people that I love them, and it means something different to every single person I tell it to. They say no two snow flakes are the same, and that's how I feel. I got my family, I got my friends, and those I'm in love with, those who are my friends that I'm not in love with, and those who might be both.

Sometimes I'm in love with C.M., like when I look into those innocent eyes. I would tell Jones this and he thought it was bullshit. Like how the fuck is C.M. innocent. He thought I was making an excuse to keep liking C.M. But I swear to God, dawg, I've seen it. More than once. More than ten times. And when I see it, I wish I could bring out the good in him and make him my man. 'Cause he's the one I really want. And I know I fucked it up with him. 'Cause we started to get close and when I started fucking some of his friends and his brother, he pushed me away. So later on, when I told him I loved him, he said, "Then why did you fuck those guys if you love me?" I guess I kept telling him, "I love you," because maybe for once he would tell me a different answer, but he never did. And I had him for awhile. I can really say he was mine for a couple of weeks. But then we go to some of these places and shit, and you know, there's some hot guys there.

I remember the first time it happened. We go to one of the bars and I start talking to this dude. He had muscles, he was so fucking hot. So then I start stroking the back of his neck and I see him smile. I kinda look around the bar and see C.M. talking with some of his homies that we met up with there and I know he didn't see me.

So I whispered in the dudes ear, "Do you have a car?" And he says, "Yes." So I was like, "Let's go there. Quick." So I led him out a different door of the bar and went to his car and we fucked real quick in his car. And it was over and I was happy 'cause I was tingling, dawg, I felt so fucking good. And since it was fast, we could get back to the bar with no one knowing we were gone. Especially not C.M. So I was straight up with the dude, I was like, "Sorry, my brother's here, and if he sees us together, he'll go nuts." So he went off somewhere and I went to the bar and acted like I never left. So then C.M. comes over and says, "Where the fuck did you go?" I said, "Just the restroom." I guess somehow C.M. didn't see that dude.

But I paid for doing this. I really fucking paid. I thought I could get around C.M. It was like, here's this guy I really like and he likes me, plus I can fuck other guys on the side and he won't know. The problem is, I ended up at another bar one night just with my best friend, she was a dancer like me. And this cute guy comes up and starts talking to me. But I'm not really that interested. But then he said he wanted to smoke me and my friend out. So we were in her car and followed him ho his crib.

Then my friend only took two hits and I was so blowed. So then she goes, "I gotta leave," And I say, "Maybe Matt here wants me to stay." And he's like, "Yeah, sure." So then, of course, we did it when my friend left and I don't know if he used protection or not. And I don't admit this to people 'cause I don't want it spread around, but you get me high and I'm horny. It really don't matter if it's shwag or KB or what it is, I just wanna get down. Jones must've figured that out at one point because one time out of nowhere-and this guy never smokes-one time out of nowhere he called me up and told me to smoke with him.

I mean, where the fuck did that come from? I knew he never bough t, almost never smoked with me and C.M., and now he invited me? I'm sorry, but that was early on when I first knew him, and I definitely wasn't into him back then. And I can think of so many times when I only talked to him on the phone to try to find C.M. or he'd invite me somewhere and I said no. What happened here, I guess, was my fault 'cause I first started telling him I loved him like two weeks after I met him. There was a few times that Jones drove me back to my house on the Northeast Side. And it was a quiet ride, neither one of us talked and all of a sudden I told him, "I love you." And he didn't say nothing. I think he looked at me real quick and then turned back to the road. He didn't say anything that time, but after that it changed. I really don't think any girl told him that before so he probably didn't know how to take it right. And I can admit that I led him on when this happened.

'Cause one time in another one of our car rides, he started crying about his grandfather who died a long time ago and I comforted him. I stroke his cheek with my fist and he was cool later on, but I don't know why he decided to act that way. That didn't help if he wanted me. I need a soldier, not a cryer. Then another time, we were in his bed and he cried again. It seemed like he made himself do this 'cause he thought he could get me that way. And this time when he cried, I'm like, "What the hell's the matter with you?"

Those early times with Jones are important because maybe things would've been different if he didn't do some of the things he did. The way I think and most girls also do, is that when they meet a guy, most of the time the guy has a chance with her. And the girl will test that guy or just sees how he acts when they're getting to know each other. Maybe she wants to see if he parties or goes out late, of course how he dresses, hair, does he have money. And then, does the guy start saying stupid shit or acting different than before.

Basically, Dr. Jones turned me off. At first, when I first knew him, that's when C.M. started taking me to Jones' house. The three of us would sleep together on Jones' bed with me in the middle, of course. But we spent a lot of other time-when that little guy who lived with Jones, whatever his name was, was yelling at us to be quiet in the morning or just to leave the house and C.M. would yell back, but anyway, we're chilling and then I would jump on C.M. and start kissing him all over his face and he'd push me away. Now, this was already after I fucked around on C.M. and now I wanted him back. But being around Jones, he didn't wanna bring that up. Instead, he was like, "I already got a girl. But that was bullshit, 'cause they already fuckin' broke up. That's like me saying I was still married, 'cause I got divorced a while ago.

The reason C.M. stayed special to me was 'cause he was my first after I got divorced. And I was his first after he and Rachel broke up. I would've given anything to go back and not do what I did to C.M., but it didn't help when he acted like he didn't give a fuck. 'Cause when he found out, he said, "Fine, we'll do other people." So I had some of his friends and then his brother. And damn, his brother's gorgous.

And Jones made some wrong moves. One time I called him up and told him I felt really lonely that night, like no one cared about me. Of course, I was at the club when I said this. So he goes, "Well why don't you come by here later. I care about you." And it was so unbelievable, dawg. I had shivers when he said that. 'Cause no one else was telling me this. C.M. wasn't telling me this. Could this be the guy? Could this be the night?

So, later on I get in bed with him and soon I put my head on his chest the whole rest of the night. And nothing happened. He didn't even make one move on me. 'Cause that's what I wanted. Maybe he felt unsure, but he shoulda tried. And again. Girls are always looking for things from guys. And if you don't deliver, you're out. So maybe this was it. Stay away from a guy who can't take charge. And I feel bad for Jones, but this is just the way women are. You can do one thing wrong and never get another chance as long as you live. And, of course, it's all about feelings, too. If I don't feel it, it can't be there. Now, if we had done something that night, things could've been a lot different. And I would never tell Jones about this probably 'cause he would think it's a stupid reason or he could've got real sad. I don't know.

Another bad move from Jones early on was when it got kinda close to Christmas time. See, C.M. called me up right before Thanksgiving and told me to go with him to Jones' parents' house where Jones was staying that night. So I'm like okay, but it was weird that we were going there that day. So we get there and go upstairs to the bedroom where Jones was waiting for us. Then all of a sudden he gave me a little box and a three page letter. So I looked at the letter for a coupla seconds and just dropped it to the ground. I don't think Jones liked this, so I wouldn't look at him. So then I open the box and there was a pretty nice watch inside but then when I tried it on, it felt all the way down my arm. So he didn't get it adjusted to fit my arm. Jones couldn't even buy a gift right for a girl and his note was long and I couldn't read his writing. But for some reason, I don't know why, I thought about it, I wanted to give him a chance. So I walked up to C.M. and whispered to him, "I wanna talk to you in that other bedroom. Let's go." So C.M. tells him to wait there and we went to that other room. So we go there and turned on the light and it was 'cause no one was in there. So right away, I was like, what do I do? And he said, "Do what you feel like." And I told him it was nice what Jones did, but I didn't feel it for him. But how do I do this without breaking his heart. I mean, I could keep the watch and not take the letter. And C.M. thought how could he know how I felt if I didn't take the letter too. But I just didn't want Jones to think he got me. If I took both things, of course he's gonna think I love him, too. And if I don't take anything, I hate him or he has no chance. And the truth is, I did want him as an option, but definitely not the only one. I wanted him to think he had a chance but not too much of one. So I decided to mix it up on him, more mixed signals, but I just could not think of another way.

So then I went back to the other bedroom and told C.M. to wait there. When I went in, Jones was sitting on a couch against the wall and he didn't say anything and looked up at me and I walked over to him and stood right in front of him and he kept sitting down. Then he reached out his arms and hugged my legs. And I thought that was weird and said, "O-Oh, I don't know what to tell you." And he just kept on not saying nothing and then he felt me trying to leave and he let go of me. Then I left the room. I took the watch but left the letter there. And me and C.M. left.

So then a couple of days later he called me and asked about the watch. And I told him I lost it. That was a lie because I threw it away right when I went home that other night. I know that's a real fucked up thing to do. Bit it was kinda his fault for not makin' sure it fit me. How the fuck could I possibly wear it? I know he spent a lot of money, but, I mean, it's fucked up, but I just felt like throwing it away.

But I did like Jones, and sometimes I thought about picking him, but it never felt totally right. Of course, he asked about it a couple of times, if I ever thought about being his girlfriend and I said yes. I thought about it and I wasn't lying.

But never enough for it to happen. You know, I hooked up with guys a lot during that time, and I didn't want a commitment. And I didn't. It's not like he's the only guy who wanted a commitment. Other guys too and I just didn't want one with anyone. And, I hate to say, but girls, especially pretty girls, have a lot more opportunities than guys do. It's true. Everyone knows that. And doing what I do for a living, there's guys everywhere. And they all want you. And I know C.M. has lots of chances, but even he has a harder time than me. And what can I say, I like sex and it happens a lot. That don't mean I'm a slut or a ho. Guys can call me that if they wan, but I have the freedom to do what I want. Today's woman has power, dawg. We have power that men can't push us around no more. I'm in charge of my life and no one tells me what to do. And I like it that way. If they don't like my lifestyle, then fuck them.

And when I want a boyfriend, I have one. And anyway, I haven't always been like this. I wasn't always a dancer, I didn't have a lot of men. I was married at a very young age and before that in high school, I only had two guys. But my marriage went bad after a couple of years and I got divorced and something about all that made me go wild. But still love my ex husband in a weird way, like I still want him but there ain't no way I'm going to go try to get him back. After we divorced, I just had an urge to experience men. And I'm not going to always live this way, but I also don't always know where my life is heading. My life changes a lot. Maybe Jones met me at the wrong time. Maybe we weren't ready for each other. And when he found out about other guys, he got jealous but not so much when I would tell him about the latest times I had been with C.M. 'Cause that's what he saw from the beginning. He was used to that. And I know for sure he respected C.M.'s game.

And see, the first time Jones ever really got mad at me is when he found out about me and Adam, and he was getting' crazy on me that night, dawg. 'Cause C.M. had told him, about it and later when were in Jones' car, he's like,"So, I heard about you and Adam. Is he good or what? … you know, I'm not good enough for you, but he is …" and again, I'm like, "It's not like that."

'Cause it wasn't like that. I wasn't trying to ruin Jones' life, but he took it that way. He assumed that I fucked everyone on earth except for him. And that ain't fuckin' true. Yeah, I fucked a lot of guys, but I didn't even fuck Shystee's room-mates, even though I fucked Shystee. I didn't give a shit about Nice Guy and he was always in that room with Daisy anyway. The other dude I hardly ever talked to, and definitely not that guy Caveman.

And other people came to the house a lot, and it's not like I fucked all them. But here we were in the car that night and Jones was demanding why I fucked Adam. And I think he was cool with Adam but he didn't respect him. I know he thought Adam was ugly 'cause he said, "Just look at that guy." So fine, I thought, I thought he was cute and he had a big dick. Sometimes that's all it is. And also, it's not like I fucked his older brother Nick. I didn't like that guy at all and I would think Jones would respect him more than Adam. And you know what, that makes me angry that Jones thinks I'm like a buffet line where everyone ges his turn. I may have been around al lot, but even I wasn't that bad.

And, plus, with Adam I was drunk and called him up like a fucking booty call. So I don't even know if I woulda done it without drinking. But seriously, think-ing about that guy's dick turned me on. It was kinda like that with C.M., 'cause his was huge, dawg. But with C.M., it's much more than physical. Those inno-cent eyes. And when he's happy he was always so great to be around, throwing out all these jokes, like sometimes I could just feel his soul, like his soul wanted more love but there was no way he would say that out loud. I mean, always acting he was a tough guy who didn't need no one. And I really thought this made him weak.

And then someone would do something to piss him off, say the wrong thing or something, and he'd be there in his room with me and Jones and sometimes just me and he would just talk, just talk on and on about all this bullshit, and I would be like, "Man, I'm tired of hearing this," and then he'd turn it on me and be like, "Yeah, you don't care about me either, bitch." And he was always calling me a bitch or a ho, and I didn't like it. I wasn't cool with it. But he didn't care. Sometimes I wonder why I kept coming around. So maybe I should partly blame myself. 'Cause despite everything he did to me, I was so fuckin' attracted to him, dawg. One time I even showed up at his house without telling him. I had Jones drive me there and wait in the car as I went around to his back porch where he and his brother was and I just told C.M. what I had to say. I told him, "I love you, okay. You're the man I want in my life. No one else. I wanted you to know this even if you don't feel the same way."

And he looked around a little bit and neither one said anything and then C.M. said, "Well, I don't feel the same way. That's just the way it is." That's all he fuckin' said. So I went back and got in Jones' car and told him to take me home. When Jones asked what happened, I told him what I had said but I wouldn't tell him what C.M. said. The only good thing that happened out of all that is that C.M. and his brother didn't laugh. 'Cause I thought they might. Narciso didn't treat me much better than C.M. He was nice, but I knew he didn't care about me, even after we had sex. I mean, he would treat me like any person who came by, not like someone who should be closer to him. But I'm pretty sure Narciso was a player, but he was real good at keeping it on the DL because he had some major involvement with a girl, and those guys got mean if you brought it up. But I had "Our Song" with Jones. It was a slow song and sounded nice and sometimes we would sing with it. There was some other ones too, but that was the main one. But sometimes I think I shouldn't have called it that. 'Cause I could tell when I did, he would smile and start thinking he had a chance with me again. And also, there was a long time where he was broke and I had money and I would buy us both food. We went to McDonald's a lot. I know he hated McDonald's but I also knew he wouldn't turn down free food. And it wasn't that bad, anyway. It was at least okay. I can't explain why I liked McDonald's, I just did.

And I also took him to "La Fruteria" where I would always get one of those roasted corn cups with with sour cream and all this other shit, I don't know what. And Jones hated this place worse than McDonald's, but he kinda liked those tortas they had. But I could be bad about those things, too. 'Cause he liked

Jack'N'the Box and I never went there with him. Or we would go to KFC and he liked Popeye's or Church's. He hated KFC, he said it was never fresh.

But then we also went to nice places like Olive Garden and Outback. But sometimes he had money and I didn't or we'd split the bill in half. Sometimes I would cook at my apartment and give him spaghetti or something. I remember the first time I did this, he looked shocked that I actually cooked. But I do like to go out to eat even though I'm really skinny.

We even stayed in hotel rooms together, me and Jones. But I knew I could trust him not to make a move because I would fight him. One thing I know about Jones is that he respected women and I don't know if he thought he'd get laid those times, but there was no way. In my mind, I knew I was gonna keep it that way, but I knew he was going to keep being confused as long as I sometimes told him other things or did certain things with him.

There were times we held hands. A lot of times. Now, I know holding hands doesn't necessarily mean you are in a relationship, but it can be a sign of closeness between a man and a woman. And maybe he judged it too seriously. Because I like taking long walks, and for awhile I would call him up and ask him to take a walk with me. And he was always eager to do it. I don't know if this was something that made him think that I was starting to have different feelings toward him or if he was just glad that I actually wanted to spend quality time with him.

'Cause I'm sure he remembered all those times I called him just to find out where C.M. was and I know he didn't like that. Or also back then I refused to hang out with him if C.M. wasn't there. He got real mad about that one time. We was in my car and me and Jones, we were supposed to meet C.M. at that restaurant, Jon's. So we get to the parking lot, right, and I drive around and I don't see his car. Then I looked from my car into the restaurant 'cause it has big windows where you can see everything. So C.M.'s not there, instead he's at Shystee's, back before everything went down, so I said, "We ain't going to Jon's, we're going back there." And that's when Jones got fuckin' pissed dawg. He starts goin' on and on about what the fuck is my problem and that I thought that I was too good for him, and told me I weren't worth a shit and I told him he was goin' psycho on me and he didn't seem to care about that. But I just didn't value him at first, and this was after I first told him I loved him.

So after a while, we started taking walks together, like every day. And a lot of times, we held hands. And his hands were pretty small, but mine we're even smaller and real skinny and soft. I loved holding his hand. I can admit it was kinda intimate. And sometimes we kissed on the lips. But only sometimes. And of course, I would see his face light up.

I think one problem was one night when we walked around the block of his parent's hause. 'Cause all of a sudden I stopped and so he stopped and told him I wanted to be in heaven with him and my mom who had died when I was only six years old. I don't know how he took it, but his eyes got real wide. But I figure he thought I was telling him that he was my soul mate and I can see why. It makes sense when someone tells someone else that they wanted them in heaven.

And I shoulda known better not to tell him like that. Don't get me wrong, I did want him in heaven with me, but not just him and my mom. I wanted all my family and cousins and shit, people like C.M. and my ex husband, it's just I wanted to include Jones in a way that would make him feel important. And he is important to me, dawg. He's so important to me, but so are a lot of people. Jones just never understood the way I think. He thinks everyone has to be one thing or another, and that just ain't true with me. Because I love people in many different ways, some as friends and lovers. And just as I mentioned my mom with Jones, I might've said my dad with someone else. Or a group of my friends could be just them and me.

'Cause really, it doesn't matter. 'Cause if this is a place of happiness, then the only way I'm happy is if it is done this way. I need a heaven of different people in different places. The reason I placed Jones with my mom is because if my mom ever met any guy I know, Jones is the one I want her to meet. Jones is the guy to take to meet your mother. If Jones knew I thought this, he probably wouldn't like it, like he's a fucking goody two shoes or something.

But it should be something he would honor and cherish. 'Cause it's always a good sign for the guy if the girl wants him to meet her parents. But yes, I didn't have my dad with my mom and Jones. I think I need to keep my dad in some other heaven rooms, but not this one. This one is for my mom and would be the best way I could ever show Jones how much I cared about him.

He became my best friend, the kind of person that is there for you, will do anything for you whenever you need him. And heaven is a place without sex, and by the time I'm dead and in heaven, I won't want sex anyway. I can think of nothing better than my best friend at my side, meeting my mother and telling her how much he has wanted to meet her. Something I noticed about Jones is that he has great conversation skills. He could talk to my mom for hours and hours for eternity. My mom really needs this. I know she's already in heaven, but it would make it an even greater heaven. That's sounds weird, but why can't it get even better than it already was.

'Cause we can't all get there at the same time. C.M. would fit somewhere, too. I don't know, dude, maybe driving around in his car and getting' blowed. Just a drive to nowhere. We don't have to start nowhere and we don't have to end up nowhere. Just driving forever, dawg. And it's heaven, so you don't have to be in one place. At the same time I'm with my mom and Jones. I'm cruising with C.M. Forever. Then I throw in the memory of me and my ex husband on my wedding night. At that point, it was the happiest day of my life. Also, Forever. I think for someone to understand heaven, you have to think of it as a place so great that anything good can happen. No more bad feelings and everything's complete. I can't have everything complete if I can only see some people sometimes in some places.

But with Jones, it's like in real life if I tell him I like something about one of his brothers, and one time I told one of his brothers that he could do me. But I know Jones thinks that I should automatically like him more than his brothers and sister. That's no problem with his sister, 'cause I don't like her. But I could say all the brothers are cute in their own way. Again, why does it have to be one thing or the other? I really don't like it that way.

But, you know, I see different thing about those brothers that attract me in different ways. Dr. Jones is so smart. He does so much in his life. He always wants to get better. The next brother, Alexander, always looks like he's in a good mood and he's funny a hell. I would think about doing him. And Stan, oh my God he's so hot. I can see why he had a girlfriend. He probably always had girlfriends. 'Cause he's so fuckin' thin, dawg. And he had such a beautiful face. I mean, he's so adorable. Like the way he talked, he talked so quiet and nice. That was so different than Dr. Jones, 'cause Jones could be loud and yellin' at me when he didn't like what I was doing. It just looked like Stan was chill, you know. And he toked all the time. God, I think about it a lot, dawg. If I could just see him naked. Just once. But then that wouldn't be enough. 'Cause then I would want to fuck him for sure. And that would've messed it up with his girlfriend.

And there was his youngest brother, Trevor. This is the brother I went to and told him I would have sex with him. The reason I did this was 'cause he was shy, so I thought he might be a virgin. And boy, did I love virgins. I was like a vampire. Not only that, but he was cute and knew how to play the guitar. See, when I told Trevor this, I was sitting next to him in the room upstairs where everyone was. The next day or whatever, Jones told me that Trevor told him about it. And I denied it, dawg, rowdy, 'cause I didn't want him to get jealous. I was like, "There was no way in hell that I told him this." And then Jones was like, "Trevor told me you did and that he would never do it because he thought I told him before that you had herpes. And I believe you told Trevor you wanted to fuck him 'cause he's the most honest person in this world." And I got pissed off that he said I was lying. But he was right, I was lying. And I got mad and said, "I did not ask your brother to fuck. And I definitely don't have herpes. "But I know you told me you did," Dr. Jones said.

"I don't know where you got that," I said. The truth is, I think I had it, but it went away. I hadn't had an outbreak in two years. And I don't know if it can go away by itself or not. It's not like I'm a doctor. But I would like to think that if you don't see it for two years, it ain't no longer there.

I'm sorry, but sometimes I have to lie to Jones for his own good. I love him a lot, but he wants things to be a certain way with me, and they just aren't. I mean, I would fuck any of his brothers before I would him and it's not 'cause I don't like him or he's ugly. It's just that I don't see him that way, I can't see him that way. No matter what, dawg. No matter what. But I need to do what it takes to keep him around as a friend. The way Jones never gave up on me, that's what I did to C.M. And C.M. was always treating me like I was a bitch. But I always looked beyond this to see those innocent eyes. Some days it was hardly there and on others that's all you saw.

They were the eyes of an Aries, and an Aries always covering himself up to protect himself. And when Aries people do this, it makes them more evil than everyone. 'Cause their same eyes can be very mean. C.M. was a big fuckin puzzle. Some days I went over and he didn't talk to me at all, other times a lot more chill. And sometimes, he was sweet on me, got romantic and flirted and before I knew it, we were fucking. Sometimes when we fucked, he made me go to the other room. To the couch after we finished. Other times, he was sweet and calm and let me sleep in the bed with him. And that's part of what it means to be a woman. Having sex to me is not just the thrusting, it's all the kissing and licking before and sleeping and closeness after. C.M. never did both and barely ever let me sleep with him. But Jones was thrilled to do both those things for me. So for awhile, C.M. was the straight up sex(which he was good at) and Jones was good with intimacy(which he was good at). I told C.M. how that worked and he laughed and thought that was stupid. And then he was like, "Damn, Precious, why you gotta fuck Jones over like that?" But I said, "He's more special than you 'cause he does that for me."

"Why don't you tell him that, then," and he just smiled. I knew I wasn't gonna tell Jones, 'cause he would just feel used or something. I mean, why do all them have to have sex with the girl or she's worthless? Like it's sex or nothing. I can admit that during this time I was having way too much sex, dawg.

It's definitely something I had to work through, but it's funny, that whole lovemaking is not something I want with anyone other than C.M. 'Cause when I do all those other guts, I leave when I am finished.

For awhile, I would tell Jones the next day when I hooked up. You know, like I did two dudes from the club or something. So the first few times I did this, he stopped me and said, "I don't wanna hear about this," so I stopped.

And see, this was happening after my best girlfriend moved and I needed him to step in and hear this stuff. But after this I knew this wasn't the person. He didn't have to tell me 'cause he still liked me. I knew that. I just thought I'd try and take our friendship in a whole new direction. He knew C.M. wouldn't listen to my shit, so why should he.

I always figured that Jones remembered everything I said to him, good or bad. One time, when all three of us was in Jones' house, I turned to both of them and thought I was giving both of them a big compliment 'cause I said, "Why can't y'all have the brain of Jones and the body of C.M.?" And, of course, both of them took this wrong, 'cause Jones said, "Great I'm not attractive and C.M. said, "I'm stupid but good looking." And I just said, "You all are so great at each one, I'm just saying you'd be the perfect man." Jones said, "I don't need any help. I'm just fine how I am," and C.M. said pretty, much the same thing. I swear to God, as much as these guys knew me, they couldn't figure me out. I will not always say things straight out, that's just how I am. And if I do, I won't explain it, so you have to figure it out. 'Cause I'll be talking to Jones and I'll say something and he'll be like, "What do you mean, What do ya mean," and I'll keep my mouth shut. It's not such a secret, I just don't feel like talking any more and trying to explain something to Jones that he should already understand. And yes, so many people think I'm stupid and whiny. Even Jones' dad talked shit about me behind my back. 'Cause it got back to me when Jones himself told me.

And it had something to do with, you know, his dad said something about, "Shotgun Shacks" and so I go, "What's a Shotgun Shack?" And his dad said something and went to the other room. And then Jones came to me later and told me how his dad thought I was stupid 'cause I didn't know what a shotgun shack was. So, what, just because I hadn't heard of something means I'm stupid.

And then Seventy Three started calling C.M.'s dog "Precious" because he said that dog was whiny like me. Man, that dog liked to whine, too. I never once heard that dog bark. Every time it made a sound, it whined like a fucking whiny bitch. I just don't understand why Seventy Three was comparing it to me. It's like, come on now, you have to know someone who bitches more than me. I don't even bitch hardly at all. I may complain sometimes, but I'm not that bad.

Seventy Three barely around me anyways, and when he is, I'm usually calm and quiet. What about his girl? He's around her all the time. She's the mother of his children. She has more to complain about than I do, like a husband who fucking leaves whenever he wants for his rap shows and gang banging and whatever else he's doing. Like he's coming home late at night a lot and what, she's not yelling at him, not bitchin' at him, asking where he was? Trying to quiet her babies. And I've seen her too, dawg, and she's ugly. I'm a lot hotter than her. So I know why he's talkin' shit. It's cause he can't have me. Word has gone far by now about my sleeping around and he thinks he can get on the gravy train. So as soon as he saw he wasn't getting anywhere with me, he gave up and that little dog was a perfect way to get back at me. And of course, Seventy Three automatically knew that C.M. loved making fun of me and I usually didn't say anything. So, then, where does this whiny bitch shit come in?

Seventy Three is just some little bitch trying to act hard. 'Cause I know for sure you can't say nothing to him without him getting pissed off. He wouldn't even joke around with anyone. And I'm the whiny bitch? And I know how this shit goes. You know, C.M. and Seventy Three just on his back porch chillin', then up comes running that stupid ass dog. And "ee-ee-ee,ee-ee———" and they don't know what the dog wants, 'cause this is the only sound she makes.

And then C.M. had to be a smart ass and pipe up, going, "This dog bitches like Precious. And then Seventy Three is real happy t jump in, thinkin' he's going to get revenge on me. Now who's being the whiny bitch? And then C.M.'s fucking with me every time I come over, telling me, "Hey, look, it's Precious the Dog, Ha-Ha."

Now, something like this shouldn't be a big deal to me, but it's one of those things that kept making me think about why I wanted C.M. so bad. You know, 'cause all those times I would go over there with Jones there, too, and then C.M. would start making fun of me and Jones would join in every time and I didn't understand why Jones did this. 'Cause he did it every time, dawg. Couldn't just once in a while he defend me? But I'm sure it's because he thought it was no big deal. Also, he would look at me and I always acted like I didn't care and sometimes I answered back and sometimes I didn't. And it's not like I woulda hooked up Jones if he defended me at those times. 'Cause he still wouldn't have had no chance. It just would've been nice for someone to step up for me. And as far as C.M., the attraction never left no matter what he did. He had that bad boy thing that girls love. But these two guys had much more bitchiness than I did.

Jones would yell at me all the time, dawg. You know, all the jealousy stuff, like he always did. But sometimes, when he thought I was being rude to him, or inconsiderate, he got just as mad. Like we went to his parent's house one time real quick for him to get something and come right back out while I waited in my car. Well, it seemed like it took him forever, so I just drove off. Next thing I know, he's calling me up while I'm driving and stupid me, I answer and he's yelling at me real fucking loud and I hung up on him. 'Cause I don't owe him no explanation.

And then later, when I didn't have a car anymore, I had him to come pick me up to hang out or take me to work. If I thought I could get someone faster, I would change my mind and have them come get me and I wouldn't tell Jones 'cause I knew for sure he would yell at me, so I wouldn't tell him I didn't need him no more. So then he'd show up and see me not there and then get pissed and leave an angry message on my phone or yell at me the next time I saw him.

And yes, I know I shouldn't have dissed him like that, but it showed him I didn't need him, 'cause I didn't. He needed me, but I didn't need him. It was a fact. The whole fuckin' time, it was fact.

So then you got Jones doing that shit to me and then C.M.'s blaming me 'cause he lost his job. He kept saying that shit and it was really pissing me off, 'cause he would be like, "I was late because of you. You kept me up late." Or, "When we hang out, you stress me out because you're bugging me and telling me shit I don't wanna hear."And, of course, there was that time that he almost killed us on the freeway after him and Jones were yelling at each other on the way to getting his check and quitting his job. And they almost got in a fight at the place and C.M. was driving like a fuckin' maniac on the way back. I was never so scared in my life. I just think we were going to die for sure. And C.M. made me sit up front, yelling about how me and Jones betrayed him and I didn't know what the fuck I did. Later on, Jones told me he thought that C.M. was just acting that night. But I don't think so.

But really, looking at all this, who's weak and who's not? I'm the little, whiny bitch, right? Then why did Jones yell at me everytime I dissed him? And why did C.M. blame me for all his problems? What about his ex and his kid? What about the work he owed his family? But no, it's my fault he quit his job. At least he has his parents. I lost my mom when I was six. And she might've been kidnapped and murdered, I don't know how she died. My dad's distant. I can call him when I want, but there's no connection. So it really feels like I have no parents at all, and I'm way too young for that. I don't even have my own kids. It really feels like I have no family. But look then at C.M. and Jones. Both their parents are alive an around them, their parents care about them and what they are doing. I would give anything for that, but I have never told this. I always kept it to myself. And you know what, Seventy Three never named the dog after me when I was around, so how big are his balls anyway? And that's another thing about me, I'm never afraid to tell anyone to their face what I really think. I did it to Jones kinda with the watch he gave me, but most of the time 'cause he just talked to me too much. You know, 'cause he'd just go on and on and it was boring as hell. It was just shit about him, like details about his life that talked about shit I wasn't interested in.

'Cause he needed to be into me. You know, asking me questions so I could tell him about my life, not the other way around. Remember, I am the woman and I'm pretty and everyone knows I'll be the one to pick who to hang out with and who to date.

I mean, dawg, I'm talking about we're in the strip club, right, and he should be smiling and hangin' like a G, right. And again, this is in the earlier times with him when I did consider him. After all, it was just me and him in that club that night. So here I am telling him he talks too much and thinks women like good conversationalists, that I should like him talking all the time. But a good conversation is both people, not just him.

I didn't really tell him that part, but I was like, "You should be glad I have the balls to tell you this straight to your face." But I don't think he went along with that at all. And around that time, in a phone call, he called me up and basically laid it out. He wanted to date me or whatever, and again, I told him straight up, that he wasn't into me enough. And again, I don't think he understood me, so in the future when stuff like this came up, I just didn't explain myself no more. Just kept my mouth shut. Didn't say shit. So he'd be like, "So, what? What do you think? Why can't you give me a chance?" But by then it was over. But I will admit I led him on so many times. It's like pretending to pour dog food in its bowl. It still comes over to see every time you do it.

Now C.M. was another matter. He was the G. Put him in a strip club or any other kind of bar, and he looks like he automatically owns it. Put him in the strip club and he's smiling and laughing like he doesn't have a care in the world. Talking about, "Hey, I like your body," or he goes to the stage and says, "Baby, why don't you come my way?" And believe me, most of the girls will and not just to get money.

That's how it started with me and C.M. 'Cause I met him at the other club. I worked at back then when I just started, right after my fucking divorce. The forst time I went on stage that night, I happened to see him at a table close to the corner, all by himself. But he looked chill with a little smile on his face, just looking around, just scoping around, not looking like he was in no hurry.

Most of these guys, especially when they are by themselves, are all zooming around the room real fast, like there ain't no girls in there. It's like we're right here right in your fucking face. Seriously, they just can't sit still. The looking around, the hand's on the table. Believe me, I can see it. I can see it from the fucking stage. You know they're nervous and this makes you nervous. And then their fucking clothes are wack, too. I mean, even if they are wearing a suit, it's wack 'cause it ain't like a G. You may see only a few G's a night, and when you see them, you know right away those are the one s you're gonna talk to 'cause they're cool, they know how to dress, and they are relaxed. So you go talk to them with a big smile on your face, and they make your day nice. You know they got money and you know they got drugs. And weed was all I ever asked. These dudes knew how it worked I'm there, so fuck everybody else, I ain't got time for them So every night on stage I was thinking these things, even though I was new. 'Cause I caught on quick because the other girls gave me a lot of tips and other things that just made sense. So the night I saw C.M. for the first time, I had only been there a week, but he was an easy choice. So I went through the stages and then went straight to him, dawg. And he was nice and friendly and talked to me like he knew me forever. Saying shit like, "So what's up, baby? You wanna chill here or what? Or I could hook you up with some kill." Right when I heard this last part, I knew I had to keep him around. We talked and then he got a coupla dances, but I just knew he had more money, but he knew not to give too much so that I would come back for more on another night. Or he might talk me into leaving with him that night. But not that night. I wanted to make him work a little harder. And I'm no sure if I wanted him sexually but I did want that kill. But it's not like I'm desperate or anything. It's not coke. I don't need it that bad. I just knew after meeting C.M., that I would have to figure out what I would give him.

This was a whole new world. At this point, my ex-husband was still my last, so I hadn't hooked up with anybody yet, definitely not someone from the club.

But I sensed that C.M. was a nice guy, like he wasn't gonna force shit like some straight up weed-for-sex deal. 'Cause that weren't gonna fly. And so he comes in three nights later and he didn't even call me so I was kinda pissed off. Like is he interested or not? So I go up to him and I'm like, "What the fuck?" but I didn't say it mean, I was kinda smiling but I wasn't real happy either. And then he was just like, "Sorry, baby, but I had a feeling you'd be here tonight, so I wanted to peep this joint like a player, Ahh-Ha-Ha, just fuckin' around." And I really just couldn't help laughing at that. 'Cause ist was funny, even though he was being a jerk. But he was so fine, though. Like his fuckin' face, dawg. Oh my God! I just wanted to melt his face in my hands.

And when I sat on him, his thighs were hard as a rock. And I could, just a little bit, feel his cock with my leg. But I needed more from him first. I needed more money and that kill he talked about. Since this was new, I hadn't started fucking these guys yet. But, you know, we're there and shit and he gets two dances again, nothing there and shit and he gets two dances again, nothing special. Then he invites me to go to a party with him, but they don't let the girls leave with any guys. They say it's a safety issue or something. But I have my car and I have the right to leave when I want. So he gave me directions to the party and I met him there.

So when I got there, right, I see C.M. and now I was happy. He was looking fine and I went up to him and hugged him and kissed him on the lips and I could smell him smelling so good, like he had some bad ass cologne, dawg.

And he had changed his clothes, wearing some fly shit. Like the white Nautica shirt and those nice ass jeans. Ooh, I just wanted to jump him. At that point, things changed. He wasn't a customer at all anymore, I wanted to know his mind. I wanted to know why he acted the way he did and said the things he did. 'Cause when you're around someone like him, you think the party never ends.

'Cause he always laughed and made jokes and how he's bringing me to a party. This was gonna be so much fun. But, you know, at that party, at some point he starts talking to some other people and then I did the same thing. And, you know, a coupla cute guys came up to me and, you know, I'm thinking about it. Why would I not? It's not like C.M. and I were together. What am I s'posed to do, tell those dudes, "Sorry, I can't even talk to you 'cause I think I might have a boyfriend?" No one, boy or girl, can ever take a chance like that. Plus, I had no idea who C.M. was talking to that night.

So after that night, I realized I had other options. C.M. was still at the top of the list, but he wasn't the only one. So a week or two goes by and he's taking me to parties and bars and I start seeing the same people again. And some of these guys were G's like C.M. So, you know, the first time I fucked someone that I met from these places was around this time. This tall dude name Dexter, who wasn't even that ghetto, invited me to his place to smoke me out. So of course I went with him, but I didn't plan on doing him. But I got so blowed that I smiled real big and melted in his couch. So Dexter sees this and moves from the chair to right next to me on the couch. And I didn't mind. Then he looks at me and starts rubbing his hand up and down my thigh and I was wearing a jean skirt so I felt his hand on my skin. So then I turned to him on my right and reached for his shirt with my left hand. I unbuttoned it a little and started stroking his chest and he smiled and he looked so cute that way. His chest was strong and smooth and hairless. I like it when a man doesn't have body hair. So he keeps rubbing my leg and slowly his hand is moving higher up and was keeping my legs a little bit spread while he did this, 'cause his hand felt yummy. Then he reached over to kiss me and we started making out. Then, before I knew, he put his finger inside my cooch and it felt hot like it was on fire. So then he goes, "Let's go to my room," and we went, did our thing, and that was it. On to the next guy or whatever. That's what started the problems with me and C.M. 'Cause the thing is, I fucked C.M. the next day, but my feelings about him changed. I just didn't look up to him the same way, before and after we did it. Doing it with that other guy showed me that a lot of guys look good like C.M. and a lot know what a girl is like. So I got greedy. I can admit that, that I got greedy. And sex with C.M. wasn't the best ever, and I didn't even know if his weed was as good ad that dude Dexter or anyone else.

But I did like C.M. I loved him and I thought I could hit it with other guys and still be into him. But after that first time we had sex, I kinda ignored him. I got with Dexter a couple more times, but that was just fuck buddies. Then, at some of these other parties, I hooked up with a coupla more guys. And finally C.M. found out and not 'cause he caught me disappearing, but because a jealous guy who couldn't hook up with me squealed on me to C.M.

So one day I go over to C.M.'s house and he's like, "Did you fuck so-and-so," and at first, I'm like, "No." And then he said, "But he told me who you done it with and when. Why would he make up something like that?" So I was stuck and I said,"Fine, okay, there was a few times where I hooked up with some of those dudes." And, man, I thought he would get really pissed, dawg. But he didn't. He just said, "Okay, we can work this out. Change up what's going on." And I was real happy when he said that. Like, hey, let's do our thing on our own, but still get together with each other. After that, I hooked up with even more guys and started going home with some of the guys from the club. C.M. did his thing, too. He started meeting a couple of girls and did his thing. But then I hooked up with C.M.'s brother and even after that his brother and I talked about dating but it never happened. I can honestly say that I didn't know C.M. would handle this, and when I told him, he acted like he didn't care. But when this happened, he stopped pursuing me and he didn't tell me why but told me some bullshit reasons which weren't true. Like he wanted his ex back or he didn't see me "that way" anymore.

The real reason was me and Narciso getting together. It was one thing for his friends to do me, but his brother, that must've really hurt him. But it's really not my fault that he couldn't tell me what's up. He couldn't communicate. All he had to say early on is, "I really like you, you know, date, be together," and I probably would've said yes. 'Cause I liked him that much. But he didn't step up. And I'm a woman. I'm a hot chick. With me, you better move while you have the chance. He should've known that.

So when he stopped being affectionate, I showered it on him. I would reach up on him and kiss him all over his face and he would push me away every time. And this went on awhile, I don't know how long and soon we were hanging out at Jones house all the time. Just like that. Going to a strange new house with strange people. And some of them didn't want us there. But C.M. didn't care about that and Jones didn't care about that, so I didn't. At that point, I was willing to go wherever C.M. took me. A lot of times, we would spend the night at Jones when C.M.'s parents kicked him out of their house. Don't ask me why.

We started going to Jones' all the time and I would write my poetry and C.M. would draw his drawings and Jones would show us his stories. And so, we're on this couch a lot, us three the only ones in the room, and I would jump onto C.M. and kiss him on his face. And Jones would look the other way like nothing was going on. I think when I first met Jones, he wasn't even interested in me. He wasn't gonna bust his ass coming after me when seeing me all over C.M. I think he started realizing that me and C.M. weren't as close as he thought after C.M. started leaving just me and Jones in the room. And then Jones got in my friend zone and I never let him out.

Maybe I should've been more clear to Jones how he didn't have a chance. I mean, I told him all the time, but still sometimes I told him he might have a chance. And it's like he remembered every word that came out of my mouth. I remember one time I was at Shystee's and then Jones happened to show up and he started saying all this smart ass shit to me, like laughing and kicking at my heels. There were only a few other people in the room, and one guy, I think it was that other roommate, was laughing at Jones saying all this shit.

And I kept telling him to stop kicking my heels and he was asking me something over and over that I didn't want to answer and finally I answered his question and left the house. Man, he pissed me off that day. And I just wanted him to give up on me, and he never did. He just always had to compare himself with the guys I fucked, like he was better. An maybe he was, but it doesn't matter, 'cause when a woman makes up her mind about these things, it usually stays that way. Especially the friends thing. Because once a woman thinks this way, it's really hard for a man to get himself out of it. 'Cause Jones tried, and honestly, he didn't come close. To him, it did seem like it came close because of the kissing and holding hands. And me takin him to movies and that night we spent at NIOSA. That was nice. It was so crowded downtown, so he took my hand so we wouldn't be separated. And C.M. was with us and told Jones and me to hold hands. When C.M. told us this, by then things were off and on. We'd hit it or I would give him a blowjob, but in public he didn't want to make us look like a couple. Of course, on that night, he was lookin for girls, so he figured if I was close to him, it would look like he was taken. But I don't even think he met one girl.

And Jones didn't care about any of that. To him, he was delighted with the closeness we had that night. I mean, we're talking about hours of holding hands. Walking and eating and drinking all around the crowded La Villita. Turning and kissing on the lips once in a while. Then we went to the Carnival area and walked around.

We saw one thing where if you throw a dart at a balloon you get a prize. The guy saw us together and thought we looked like a good couple but he was probably just checking me out. But anyway, Jones ain't doing too good with those balloons, so the dude moved them closer and made them worth more. So then, Jones spent eight dollars and the dude showed him what he could get and told him, "Why don't you let your lady pick it out." When I heard this, I decided to go along with it because I didn't want to ruin the mood of the night. And I think maybe somehow Jones took this the right way. 'Cause for the whole night after this, he never once said, "Are you my girlfriend?" or anything like that. So maybe by this time, he was starting to give up.

So when I picked something out, I picked a small, stuffed clown. It looked cute. I thought Jones was gonna laugh, but he didn't. And I hugged him tight, like I never did before, arms tight around his neck and pressing my face next to his and we told each other we loved each other. But really, after all this, he still really didn't have a chance. I wish there was a better way I could express my love of Jones. A way where sex is not important. That I value him just as much as C.M. 'Cause I really do. But Jones just has to act like a typical man, just sex on the brain. I need a man in my life who I want in my soul and not in my body. He can go find another girl, I don't care, but I wanna piece of his soul that no one else can have except me. I don't tell these things to people because I knew they wouldn't understand. They'd think I'm crazy and stupid. But I'm greedy. I want from men that I can grab for me only. I had trouble cheating in the past even when I was married. I don't know. Maybe I shouldn't have got married since I got divorced anyway. But I used to really believe in the power of love. That it could solve anything. But it doesn't. Even when you are in love, there's problems somewhere. And sometimes when I want to hit it with a guy, I do it whether I have a man or not. Someday I'm really gonna have to change, but right now this is the woman I am. And it's not like other chicks don't do this. The only difference between me and these other women is that they hide it and I don't. I'm not dishonest or patient enough to make up stories. Part of the power of being a woman is standing strong when people don't like what you do. I don't hide being a stripper and I don't hide being with a lot of men. So I say take it or leave it. And if you're a guy and you wanna approach me, I'll see what you got and if you're good enough. If anything, Jones is much more than good enough. He's perfect. I would tell him that all the time. He was really perfect, dawg. There was nothing wrong with him. And he'd be like, "Well if I'm so perfect, why don't you want me?" And knowing I couldn't explain my real reason, I would say, "I'm sorry, I just can't do it." And then he finally dropped it after he asked it a few more times. 'Cause I know he'll think my real reason is bullshit. But I swear it's not, dawg. And it's funny, we were on so many long car rides together that we had a chance to have some really long talks. When I rode with C.M. in his car, we didn't talk about shit with his bass pumping and him flowin' or rapping along or whatever you wanna call it. I would try it too in his car, but I never was good at it.

But in Jones' car we talked. Once in a while, one of "our songs" would come on and we would listen or sing and then when it ended, we started talking. It's funny, 'cause in C.M.'s car it was always rap and in Jones car it was always rock and I liked both. And the ring tones on my cell phone were always R&B. So you could say I like all kinds of music, but not country, just everything else. A lot of people say that shit, that they like all kinds of music, and then they don't.

And it's not just music. C.M. and Jones are very different from each other. C.M.'s flashy. Leather seats in his car, pimped out house and it's clean, nice TV, nice back porch, and he had musical instruments and a weight set in his backyard. But he hardly ever had a job. I think he also worked with his dad. He was probably selling, too. I liked that track lighting in his room. I never saw that in anyone else's house, even rich people's houses. And that's one thing about women that a lot of men don't know. Women notice the little things, and when the little things are done right, they are impressed. Most people would say, "Big deal. A bunch lights that get dimmer or brighter." But really, dawg, when you look at how clean the room is, it's a nice bed that is always made with nice TV and an nice chair, plus he smokes me out and the track lights give it a pimp touch. I think if I was already a real estate agent, I would be real happy to show this house. It's pretty small, but pimped out pretty good. And it's so comfortable in there, never hot. But then there are things like he fucking plays video games the whole time I'm there and I don't play them 'cause they're fucking boring. And then watching all that National Geographic shit. And then sometimes when Jones is also there with me, him and C.M start talking about all this boring ass shit, I don't even know what, and then I'm laying face down on the bed while they talked and finally I just go, "You guys are dorks." 'Cause they're dorks. But I love them so much. I love my dorks. 'Cause they're funny, too. Like they don't care how weird they sound. Making corny jokes and shit.

We were getting real close. Like the three of us could say anything we wanted to each other. That's what shows how close people are. We weren't trying to hide things or make each other feel better. But this wasn't always good. Like when C.M. and Jones ended their friendship. And times when I stopped being Jones' or C.M.'s friend or they stopped being friends with me. But we always made up. Always, dawg. And if they had had time in the end, Jones and C.M. would'be made up, too. That's how it always was from beginning to end. Those were my boys.

And C.M.'s bed was nice and comfortable and it felt cozy after me and him made love. But most of the time, he made me go to the couch in the other room and it was uncomfortable and I had to sleep alone. But sometimes we snuggled afterwards and this was heaven. 'Cause I would grasp him so hard it felt like I was crushing his ribs. And then the next day, he would smile and say, "Damn, girl, you bruised me." And, you know, I think about that stuff and I wonder why it couldn't always be like that. I mean, why was he most of the time acting like a jerk at me. I didn't fucking deserve that. Or times when Jones was also hanging out. And even in front of Jones, C.M. would say something nice and polite to me, or even compliment me a little and Jones wouldn't even laugh at him. I think even Jones wanted C.M. to treat me better but I'm pretty sure he never went to him about it.

A lot of the time when me and C.M. were hitting it, he'd grab my ass real hard with his fingernails. I don't know what he was trying to prove when he did this, like he thought it made him more manly, but it didn't 'cause the technique was bad. He needed that soft touch that he sometimes did and he needed to do it every time.

But there were times when he wanted to go at it and I turned him down. Like if I was mad at him or I wasn't in the mood. And then later on I would tell this to Jones and I don't think he believed me because C.M. never said anything about it. Also, Jones had the idea that I was so desparate for C.M. that there was no way in hell that I could possibly reject him.

Jones was a pretty jealous guy. He tried to play it off about the guys I fucked, but I could see in his eyes that he got sad or like if he just didn't wanna hear it. After awhile, I almost never told him about the sex I had, and that seemed to be what he wanted. But that's not what I wanted for me and Jones. But I should've known better. He liked me a lot, so it had to be a heartbreak when I told him these stories. But I needed someone to tell it too because my best friend moved, so I didn't have her to tell it to anymore. And I guess if he couldn't have me the way he wanted, then I couldn't have him the way I wanted. But after thinking about it, it was better this way, 'cause it made us real about each other. He didn't pretend to like my sex stories and I was honest to him about a lot of things. Even though I led him on, I also give him good, honest tips that would help him get a girlfriend. And I did that for him a lot. I remember one talk with Jones and it got pretty heated and loud and angry. 'Cause I thought he was disrespecting me. I mean, I thought so. And I don't know how we got on this topic, but of course it was one of our arguments where he just couldn't figure out why I wouldn't be his girl. I mean, for God's sake, why did we have to keep having this discussion? And by the time this one happened, we had already gone over this plenty of times. And mainly, I wasn't giving him the answer he wanted, as if he was so confused and that I owed him the right answer, whatever that was. And I don't owe nothing to no one; I have that right as a woman.

But this argument was different because we really told each other what exactly we wanted from each other for the first time. I still didn't tell him exactly why he couldn't have me, I just told him what I wanted him to be to me. 'Cause I said, "I want you as a friend, and that will never change. You know, and you should see it the same way. 'Cause there's so many other girls out there and you can get those girls. So worry about that and if you understand how I feel, you should have no problem."

Because that's really how I felt. I wasn't bullshitting him. I just wanted to make my life more simple and makes things with Jones easy, also. What the hell is wrong with that? I mean, I really wanted to do it that way for Jones' benefit, not just my own. 'Cause I know what it feels like to want someone who doesn't want you, and C.M. is not the only one that I thought this way about, just the most important. So I told Jones, "Why can't we just enjoy a friendship where you're not trying to get with me." 'Cause I really couldn't understand why he didn't just drop it. But then I can say that he gave a good reason. He goes, "Yes, it would be nice if I could end my feelings for you and we're just friends who never try to hook up. But as long as I've know you, my feelings have never faded. I started liking you way in the beginning and it never stopped. I tried to make it stop, but it didn't. I know it sucks for you that I can't let it go, but how do you think I feel? I'm not the kind of person that lies to myself, so I have to acknowledge in my heart that I will never stop being in love with you. Never. I already know this for as long as I live. And it's unfair that'—"

And then I interrupted, "But I don't understand why you have to stick with that—"

"Let me finish, please. It's unfair that I'm the one who has to change the way I truly feel so that I can make you comfortable. I have the right to feel the way I do, just as you get to do the same thing. I realize you don't have feelings for me, but you need to realize that this is not going to change for me, whether you like it or not. I can't turn this off like a faucet. If it goes away, that's one thing. But there is no way I can make it go away. And I believe there is no way it will go away. Don't get confused. This isn't fun for me. It's not fun loving a girl who doesn't love me back. But I accept it and I try to deal with it. But just the same, you have to deal with the fact that I want you in this way and that if we keep hanging out all the time like we already do, that this will always be there. This isn't a crush anymore, okay. You're not some flavor of the month. This thing is long lasting 'cause I now know you so well. Nothing you do anymore surprises me, and the way you are, like your mannerisms, turn me on. You're cute and sexy, but sometimes I get angry about this situation and sometimes I don't like the way you act when you get all selfish and shit—"

And I was like, "Jones—"

"Hold on. Hold on. What I need from you is to accept what I'm telling you. You have to accept that this is how it goes from my end, because by now I guess I have to deal with the fact that you do not want me that way."

So then he stops talking and we're both quiet for a few seconds, "Okay, okay," I said. "Let's just go in there tonight, enjoy each other's company, and have a good time. We can be with each other the whole time since I am not working. So we went inside and I paid his cover and bought him a coupla drinks. Then, when we went in there, I introduced him to one of my friends that was working that night. Then me and her started to put on a show for Jones. You know, all rubbing up and feeling on each other. I'm sure he wanted us to kiss, but we didn't. Then my friend went on stage and went over to Jones and sat on his lap like as if I was working.

And I would say we were there another two hours. And I had my arm around him and I started rubbing his back and he put his hand on my thigh and we would hug real tight like we had to to survive or something. I wanted to give him something that night. I wanted to make him feel special, that we can be affectionate without being lovers. I didn't tell him this, but I think he knew what I was doing. Later on, when we went home, we stayed quiet and enjoyed each other's company. When we got to my house, I didn't even hug him and he didn't even try to hug me, as if he understood that we didn't have to do this.

Man, just like with C.M. why couldn't things be like this all the time? Just a quiet night with Jones not trying to get all up on me or ask me all these goddamn questions of why I wasn't with him.

And it's not like he was just trying with me. He started hanging out with Daisy a whole lot. There aint nothin' special about her. She had big titties. That's the only reason men liked her. It had to be the only reason. 'Cause she acted stupid all the times I was around her. For one thing, why was she always in Nice Guy's room? I mean, come on, I'm not stupid. They were not just sharing a bed. I mean, I wonder how many times a day they hit it. 'Cause they were in there a lot, dawg.

Sometimes Nice Guy would come out of the room to watch TV or smoke or do Crystal, then go back in there. I only saw Daisy come out of there twice and she couldn't even fuckin' talk straight. Don't get me wrong. She and I had our moments. Things could get real wild at Shystee's. We decided one day to do a train on Daisy and it was C.M., me and Adam waiting to take our turns and we all got naked in another room and we were just about to do it, right, and Nice Guy comes in and makes us leave. 'Cause I got real horny just from being naked and I looked at her naked laying in the bed with her giant tits. I ain't no lesbian but I wanted to taste her all over. And man was I ready and our buzz had to be killed by Nice Guy. Then another time at that New Years party, we felt on each other and I looked in her eyes and her eyes looked lost. That was the night I broke that stupid elephant when me and Daisy weren't watching what we were doing. I mean, I heard that fag yell earlier when he told us to be careful. I think he jinxed us. And I already hate fags anyway. I think they're just acting that way 'cause they are tired of the way women are. So they think if they try out other guys they'd be happier. And I don't see how they can be. Girl on girl is different 'cause we are built that way, with soft skin and how we cares each other. Two guys are gross. Women don't even want to see that.

And I hate blacks. I get a lot of shit for being racist like this. C.M. gives me a lot of shit. One time he took me to one of his friend's house and there were some black dudes there. C.M. said that they were pretty hard but I didn't care, what are they gonna do, hit me in the face? Anyway, one of them keeps asking me questions like he is trying to get with me. So I just gave him short answers the whole time he talked to me. Then another black guy was like, "Hey, baby, what's your problem?" And I didn't like him calling me baby. I'll even let Jones call me baby sometimes, but it just felt like he wanted something from me, that he wanted my body. I mean, who doesn't when C.M. is probably telling these guys how much of a slut I am ahead of time, then he brings me around to show me to everyone. And I won't fuck a black guy. I don't care if that is racist or not. Most of the time I think they are dirty. Asians, Mexicans and whites are another story. Especially Asians. Everyone thinks they have small dicks, but that doesn't mater to me. Because they know what they're doing. I can have an orgasm with an Asian better than I can with C.M., especially when C.M. is selfish in bed. Most men don't give a shit if a woman has an orgasm or not. And I've done some Asians, so I know. One of my ex's is Asian and I always had one with him. Sometimes I wonder if Jones could've done it and maybe he could've. But doing it with Jones, the idea never felt right. Like as if no matter what he could offer me, it wasn't enough. It doesn't make sense and I didn't plan it that way, but the more time went on, the less I wanted to do him.

'Cause shit builds up. Knowing him a long time and hanging out with him all the time, and then all of that time not having sex, it made me nervous. 'Cause I knew that it would make things different. And also it was so far away from what we were. And when I think about how he didn't have a chance with me, I meant more in a relationship. But one time I did consider having sex with him if he paid me like $200 or something. You know, a one time only thing. And I don't care if people think I'm a ho 'cause of shit like this, it's not like I do this all the time. I barely ever did something like this, but I needed the money for rent and I thought maybe this would shut Jones up. And I was right about to call Jones when another friend of mine called and I told this friend that I needed money but not about how I'd get this done with Jones; so then this other friend offered to give me that money and I didn't have to have sex with this guy 'cause he offered without me even asking him.

So because of this, I never called Jones that night and he never knew what happened. 'Cause this other friend, Samuel, didn't even know C.M. or Jones. And, of course I didn't tell any of this to C.M. because I knew for sure he would tell Jones.

Could you fucking imagine if Jones had heard about it? He'd go psycho on me, I know it. You know, 'cause Jones would get pissed at me, but he never once hit me. But I really fucking believe he probably would've hit me this time 'cause he would've lost that chance to get with me and probably never have one again. And, believe me, he would've had no problem paying for it. He even offered in the past a few times and I would give him a mean look or tell him no fucking way, 'cause I really don't do this shit. And I definitely won't do that for a friend. I mean, I know I was going to offer him that one time, but I was desparate for money and I really wanted to make his day, not just to get him off my back, like I was hoping, but also so that when we had sex that he would be happy forever, like the rest of his life. That's probably a pretty stupid thing to think, like if you figure that many years from now, he might even forget that it happened. Plus, there's more to life than sex. With all the sex I have, even I believe in that.

And, you know, Jones and I would talk and he'd say shit like, "Man, you have it so good, getting' laid whenever you want, I wish I could get that much action," and I'd get pissed and go, "It's not as great as you think. Some days I'm miserable. I'm not having fun living this way."

"So, then, why in the fuck are you doing it?"

"I don't know. Why the fuck do I have to have an answer for you all the time?

"Because we're friends. Can't we talk about this shit?"

"I don't see why. When I used to tell you shit, you got pissed off and said you didn't want to hear it." And he was like, "Well, you were misunderstanding me, 'cause I don't need porno details, but, you know, your lifestyle—"

"You know what, I don't have to tell you nothing at all if I don't want to. As a woman—" And then he interrupted, "Why you always gotta throw that in my face? You think women are better than men?"

"No, but I shouldn't be forced to tell things I don't wanna say." But I wasn't lying to him. I was miserable. I didn't enjoy the sex. I needed it. And when it was done, I needed it again. I couldn't solve this problem at all until Miller came along. Everything changed in my life when he became my boyfriend. I felt more stable and settled down. Being with Miller made me want to stay at home instead of hunting guys down. And sex with him actually meant something. I felt a connection of souls like I never felt since my ex husband.

And, of course, the first time I went to C.M.'s with Jones there, they were making fun of Miller, 'cause they knew what he looked like, calling him ugly and fat. And then Jones told me straight up that I used to tell him all the time that if he lost weight and colored his gray hair black, that I would do him. And I did say that. So he felt that Miller was fatter than him, so what the fuck? Again, he always thought that I had to explain everything I did to him. And that's bullshit, 'cause I have the right to not answer these fucking questions if I don't want to, and I swear to God, he never learned that. But after that, neither C.M. or Jones ever talked about Miller. Even if I brought him up. I still kept hanging out with them separate from Miller and I'm sure that made them both happy. I was very surprised that Jones never talked about him knowing how he was so curious about my sex life all the time. I think when Jones realized that I was finally in a real relationship, he finally understood for the first time that he had no chance.

And that's just the way it had to be. I felt bad for him, but I gotta take care of myself. And he didn't cry about, at least that. He was probably thinking that he couldn't wait me out, and to be honest, this way was better for him anyway.

It also surprised me that C.M. wouldn't talk about Miller, either. I mean, he didn't even make fun of Miller at all after that first time when him and Jones did. The most I would hear from C.M. is if I was at his crib or whatever and I would say something like, "Ooh, I miss my baby," and he'd be like, "Whatever, dawg, why the fuck you think I wanna hear that?" And C.M. wasn't jealous, he just didn't give a shit. And if Jones was there, he wouldn't say nothing. So I was thinking, damn, I shoulda got a boyfriend a long time ago just to shut Jones up.

But even from the beginning with Miller, I was open to different things. Like maybe I'd let C.M. hit it once in a while. And I was still dancing. Things could happen at the club or somewhere else. I had a felling about Miller, that maybe I could get away with something, but I was really trying hard to keep this shit out of my head. I didn't wasn't to screw him over. He's a sweet guy and if I messed up, it would be real hard to find someone else that good. And C.M. and Jones both didn't get a long enough chance to see Miller and me together or even to get to know him enough. And they acted different after me and Miller got together, but they were trying to make it the same as the past. I know they thought this relationship was bullshit, I think mainly because they didn't see it long enough. But I'm sure they also thought that I couldn't keep a guy around. I wanted to prove that I could, especially to C.M. He couldn't call me a ho if I was committed to one guy. And maybe he would fall for me if he thought I weren't available no more.

But when I got with Miller, I didn't need C.M. for sex for the first time in a long time, like when we first met. C.M. was wrapped around my little finger back then and then he turned it around on me, so I thought it was my turn again.

At first when I was with Miller, C.M. started calling more and when I answered, he almost didn't know what to say.

Me and Miller had only been together a couple of weeks when C.M. and Jones stopped being friends on New Year's. And then I checked a message on my phone from like 1 A.M. from a number I didn't know and it was Jones leaving the message. And he left a long one too, dawg. He was talking about how horrible the night went and C.M. telling him to do something that he didn't want to do. And they went to Jones' friend's party and the chick they brought with them crashed on a chair and C.M. and Jones had an argument in the backyard. Jones told me that they talked quietly the whole time but C.M. told Jones that he never did nothing for him for that business C.M. was running, but Jones told me that he did a lot like get interviews for him and C.M. said that didn't mean shit to him. Then Jones called C.M. a liar so C.M. got pissed and told Jones he wasn't his friend no more and went inside and woke up that chick and left the party. And Jones spent the night at that place 'cause C.M. was the one who drove and C.M. told them he was coming back for Jones but he never did. But Jones already knew C.M. wouldn't come back. 'Cause why would he go all the way back there after he said they weren't friends no more? That's how C.M. works. If he wants to scare you, he'll try. So Jones left that message and I called that number at four in the morning and I was furious. 'Cause when I heard the message, I knew right away to believe Jones because I know what C.M. can do and I don't think he was in his right mind. So I heard the message, called him up and yelled at him and he said, "Man, what the fuck," or something like that an hung up. So when I called Jones, I wanted him to know I had his back.

Jones was happy to hear this from me, especially since he probably thought that I would stop being C.M.'s friend and I might've said this, but after a few days, I was talking to C.M. again and Jones and it was early on with me an Miller, so I had enough time to hang out with all three, but I had to do it separate from each other. I didn't like this at all. I mean, I could deal with keeping Miller away from the other two, but I couldn't do that with C.M. and Jones. I felt the three of us needed to be together again and I hated going back and forth between them and them talking shit about each other, a lot. I mean, what the fuck am I s'posed to say? Do I have to take both their sides?

After a little while, Jones realized I was hanging out with C.M. again, just as much as I always did. The problem is, Jones thought I was thinking about C.M. the way he was, but I patched things up with C.M. a couple of days after yelling at him on the phone. And it's not like C.M. apologized, 'cause he didn't, but I just couldn't hold a grudge against him because he didn't do nothing to me. So because of that, I couldn't really feel the anger that Jones felt, and I didn't want to feel it, either. So many times between the three of us, we'd get mad and someone stopped being friends with someone else, but we always forgot about it after a few days and were cool again. This time was different. Both of my boys now became enemies and it looked like it would never change. So I knew that the only person who could save our friendship was me. So, I would say that starting a week after hanging out with C.M. again, I would call Jones and say, "Come on, just come here to C.M.'s crib and hang out. We're having a good time here." And he was like, "Are you fucking kidding me? I ain't going near there after what he did." And I said, "You need to forgive him, Jones. You're a Christian, aren't you?"

"Yeah, but I gotta protect myself."

"Well he's not going to do anything to you." I would even tell him that C.M. wanted to see him again, but he didn't believe me. And I wasn't lying about that either. One day, I was at C.M.'s place and we had a long talk. I told him, in case he didn't remember, that he was the one that ended the friendship. And he said that of course he remembered it, but didn't know why he said it, but probably some of the drugs he was on. He also knew that Jones didn't understand this, so it didn't take long for him to think that they could work this out.

Jones was a very different story. He was very sure that he would never talk to him again. I had to figure out a way to get Jones to go to C.M. 'cause me and C.M. both did not want to force this on Jones. So I would get Jones to drive me to C.M.'s house for any stupid reason I could think of, like me leaving something there or I had to tell him something 'cause my phone battery was dead. Most of the time these were lies just to get him to go there so that I could ask him to go inside with me and that C.M. wanted to see him. But he just wouldn't go in, dawg.

One time it was so bad that Jones waited in his car while I went inside. A little bit after, C.M. went to get something from his car, which was real close to Jones' car. C.M. told me later that they were only ten feet apart and he looked out of the corner of his eye and saw Jones looking straight ahead. Then after that, Jones said C.M. didn't look at him either. I told Miller about this shit during the weeks it was happening and he was cool about it 'cause he didn't get jealous like I thought he would, but would jus smile and say how he knew we would all three would be friends again.

But during this time, I found different things to do with my two boys. I told Jones that he was my best friend, and I meant it, too. 'Cause Jones never really did anything bad to me, dawg. You know, we had a lot of arguments, but we always worked it out. And he had that special place in my heart that even C.M. couldn't get near. But even though he was my best friend he was still just a friend. When I told him around New Years, he smiled real big like it meant more than a regular friend. And it did mean more. I wish I could've expressed to him in exactly the right words how I felt about him. There was one night when we were staying at C.M.'s crib when me and Jones held each other real tight and I told him everything in his ear. I told him I loved him, I cared about him; I told him I'd be there for him forever. That no matter what, I was there. And I went on for like half an hour. So, you could say I told him everything I needed to on that day but I'm not sure if he was awake the whole time or if he couldn't hear everything I said. And I'm the type of person who hates repeating themselves. I can only hope that Jones really knew, 'cause then he could think better of me, not that I was teasing him or that I'm a slut and I would hope that he started to see me as a person and not a sex object.

So, when this shit was going on, I started taking Jones to the movies with me, and he was broke during this time, so I paid again. During this time my boyfriend was cool with this. I think he had a strong feeling that nothing was going on with me and Jones. And again, sometimes we held hands, but inside the theater itself, we weren't doing anything. In this period of weeks, I took Jones to a lot of movies. Some were good and some sucked. He always thought it was funny that I liked horror movies because he said that most chicks couldn't handle that stuff. And I'm sure that part of him was thinking about how C.M. would laugh, sometimes in front of me and Jones and other times just to Jones, about how he called me Satan. I didn't really get offended because I think he did that with every girl he knew and then he's number them, like, "Satan No.1, Satan No.2 ..." and on like that.

I also took Jones to eat at some nice restaurants. Vietnamese, Chinese, but even chicken and fast food hamburgers. And he never complained, he was happy to get a free meal. I never did those kinds of things with C.M. during this time 'cause he didn't want it. Sometimes he asked for cash and I didn't lilke this but I wanted to keep hanging out with him. And I tried really hard during this time to stay true to Miller, 'cause I really cared about him, but C.M. was that Wildman you really want to get in bed with. That never changed. So sometime in the middle of all this craziness, with a new boyfriend and Jones and C.M. not talking to each other, all of a sudden one night at C.M.'s crib, he wanted some, I gave in. I gave him a fucking blow job and felt so guilty afterwards, that I just fuckin' left, without saying nothing.

So when I got home that night, the first thing I did was call Mller and show him how much I loved him by everything I said. And I was very deep about it, dawg. Very deep. 'Cause I told him that I never met anyone like him, that he was so caring and lovable and sweet. And I wasn't sure I was worth his love and I wouldn't be surprised if he found someone better than me. I was almost crying, dawg, and I don't cry a lot. 'Cause I had to prove to myself that I wanted Miller, even after now that I had cheated on him. And of course, he is a great guy, going, "I love you so much, baby. I wanna take care of you. You know that I'm not too good for you." After he said this, I decided to go to his house that night, and I like to say in this case we made love and this time is when I felt his soul. So I stayed with him three more straight days. And we hit it so many times and I didn't want it to stop. He called into work a couple of those days and it's hard to explain, but it's one of those feelings where you're in a real comfortable room lay-ing on a nice soft bed and you just want to stretch your legs real hard and then curl your toes and feet inward like a cat. And you never want to get out of that bed.

In all those three days, I think we left the house twice to get something to eat. Other times we cooked or ordered a pizza or Chinese. I could say that my guilt over my cheating with C.M. left after this. Because I gave myself completely to Miller, it made up for what I did. I was okay now. 'Cause all his actions came back to him. He could've let me stay in bed all those times instead of kicking me to the couch like he did. Or just show at least a little love or appreciation. During this wonderful time with Miller, Jones and C.M. both called and I never answered, 'cause there ain't no way I was gonna let anything kill my mood. And after these three days, I moved in with Miller. And me being a stripper, I can go in to work whenever I want. I can take two straight weeks off if I want. So for a few weeks I hardly worked and when Miller would come in from his job, I just felt so happy to see him. I mean, I really just felt it. I didn't have to make it that way. And so many times we made love, and he knew how to do it right. Older men are s'posed to be better in bed 'cause of all their experience, and he was. He was older than Jones and Jones was a lot older than me. Besides, I never really cared about age to begin with. Well, after I moved in with Miller, I started answering Jones' and C.M.'s phone calls again. And, no surprise, I didn't like what they told me about moving in with Miller. C.M. was saying shit like, "You just did this to feel better about cheating with me. And you'll cheat on him more. I know you will." And Jones was kinda jealous, going, "How's this guy better than me. Why'd you choose this guy," and I didn't answer him 'cause I don't owe him that fucking answer. I get with a guy for my personal reasons and that's the way it is. And sometimes it's 'cause it's a feeling I have, not something I can explain. And also, no reason would've been good enough for Jones', so I might as well bother him by not telling him.

But pretty soon after I moved in with Miller, they didn't call as much and didn't even bug me about Miller any more. Jones even laid off. But they still hadn't forgiven each other and started to hang out more with other friends.

C.M. told me he was going to Nick's and Adam's a lot, with Ginger and some others moving in there. Jones told me he never felt comfortable over there any-way. Jones was hanging out with dudes I never met, so it seemed like we were all three of us starting to go our own way. I knew the early going with Miller would still be great, but I didn't know how long I could hold on without looking around at other guys. I was so used to that by now. How do I train myself to stay true and still be happy? I was willing sacrifice a lot to stay with Miller, but it wouldn't always be fun. The time seemed right to stop living like I was in an orgy. To do what responsible women do .Build a life, hopefully with this man and start working to be a real estate agent. Not be C.M.'s whore or whatever he thinks I am to him. Stop hunting down weed and coke all the time like I'm used to doing now. Stay sober so I won't let people down, especially Miller. I built him up so much in my mind, like he's perfect. Of course, I'm sure he can't be perfect, but he's perfect for me. Maybe I want kids someday. I can't be doing drugs with a kid around. So if I got rid of all my past friends, settle down with Miller, and make some new ones from work, at the church, or with my neighbors, I could start doing the right things and live a normal life. So my life was building with Miller and Jones and C.M. started to disappear.

CHAPTER 2

▼

It was strange when I heard about it, 'cause Daisy's the one who told me about it. You know, my number was on her cell phone, so when she found out she told me. She knew how close I was to Jones and C.M. She was kinda stalling a bit, but when she could finally say the whole thing, I just fucking screamed, dawg. 'Cause this wasn't on the news. I guess the news just shows what it feels like showing. And also, neither hung out much with Daisy anymore, but it did happen at Nick and Adam's house, this much she knew. And those are all those dudes she knew from high school and when we all knew each other from Shystee's house.

The only problem with Daisy's phone call is that she couldn't tell me exactly who did what and I didn't know if she was covering for them or what. For awhile after the attack on C.M., Shystee left the city and people thought he might be in Florida or Chicago or God knows what. But sometimes C.M. heard from other homies he knew that Shystee was actually making visits to town, a lot. And C.M. didn't like the idea that some of them were s'posed to have his back, dawg, and they're lettin' Shystee stay with him. And I've always known him to be that way, you know, you can't be in the middle, you know, like his way or the highway. So when he said that Nick and Adam might be hiding out Shystee, that he'd keep and eye open without making it obvious what he was trying to do. You know, between Shystee's attack and C.M. and Jones getting' killed was a real long time. I don't even know how long, just a really long time. And I think he was getting obsessed, 'cause he talked about it so much.

And when you think about it, the only one who really had C.M.'s back for sure that night was Jones. Now I wasn't there that night, but I heard from other people who were. How he stood up to Shystee in front of everyone when he would not give Shystee C.M.'s cap when he asked for it. Believe me, it became well known, and I'm not sure if Jones even knew that all those people knew and talked about it later. He probably thought no one cared.

I mean, how did C.M. decide to go over there in the first place? He admitted that he really didn't trust those guys anymore, but how would he ever know for sure anyway. The whole time I knew him, C.M. didn't make the right choices. He was taking risks that he shouldn't never have taken. Why was it so fucking important to him to keep hanging out with these guys? He had plenty of friends. He didn't have to do it. And even worse, sometimes he would take Jones with him. The fact is, I know about these visits, and neither C.M. or Jones complained about it.

So maybe I should admit that I stopped worrying about it, too. 'Cause maybe the stories about Shystee showing up again weren't true. Maybe some of these other cats just told that shit to C.M. so that they could piss him off and laugh at him behind his back later. I loved C.M. so much, dawg, so much that I hurt even if I wasn't sure if he was hurt or not. Like a pain in my chest, not just my mind. 'Cause how could these fuckers want more from him then they already had. They damaged his head and put him in the hospital; why couldn't they just leave it at that? And all I can think about is how loyal these motherfuckers had to be to Shystee. Why is Shystee worth all that? Did he pay them? An d just 'cause Daisy called me doesn't mean she was doing the right thing. Fuck, man, she probably knew every last person involved, so she didn't name no one. She coulda done that so she wouldn't be put in jail or because these assholes she had known her whole fucking life, she didn't want to piss them off.

And, believe me, there are some things that point right at Daisy, a coupla things that Jones told me.

One was the night when Shystee hit C.M. with the golf club. Daisy and Jones were hanging out somewhere and got the call and when they got there and a bunch of people were hanging outside and of course, Jones wouldn't give Shystee C.M.'s cap and chain that Adam had gave him when Daisy and Jones showed up there, so he kicked Jones out but kept Daisy inside with him. And Jones said she was in there a long time with him, dawg, with his stepdad going crazy and yelling in there.

How would any of us know what they said to each other that night. They coulda talked about anything. Maybe he convinced her it was self defense and said to watch what Jones and C.M. were saying about him or planned to do about him if he showed up in town again. 'Cause right away Shystee knew that

Daisy was the only one getting close to C.M. and Jones and since they knew each other for so long, that was more important.

The thing is, I thought of these things based on what Jones told me. I took what he said and thought about it, 'cause Jones was not suspicious and C.M. was not even suspicious of her, dawg. I mean, they trusted this girl way too much, and to be honest, they hardly knew her.

About two weeks after the attack, Jones told me how he met up with Daisy and a couple of her girlfriends at a bar. But when he showed up, Shystee was there and he was shocked. Pretty soon he noticed that Shystee wouldn't look at him and was really just talking to Daisy the whole time and they were playing pool, but Jones just watched and drank a beer and Jones told me he was pissed off. So he finished his beer and just got up and left the bar without saying good-bye and he was almost at his car when Daisy and her two girlfriends went over and Daisy apologized that she didn't know Shystee would come and she pretty much begged him not to tell C.M. that this had happened and he didn't, mainly because he didn't want C.M. to think that he betrayed him, not to cover Daisy's ass.

And the thing about this is that Jones told me this story just one time, and he kept telling me not to tell C.M. and that the only reason he told me was 'cause he really had to get it off his chest. He said he felt real guilty about it and he even said he wished it never happened and that he could forget it happened. And sometimes I wonder if he did forget, 'cause he never said anything to me about it, and I know he didn't tell C.M., 'cause C.M. definitely would've told me.

Plus, I'm pretty damn sure that Shystee didn't accidentally show up at that bar that night. And if he didn't, why the fuck did Daisy invite Jones. Jones told me that when he stormed off to the parking lot and the girls came after him, he said they had a look like they all three wanted to jump him and have their way with him. I gues that was the good thing that happened to him that night. But he never did get jumped.

But during this time, C.M. is right that I didn't do him right. And I can look back and I can admit it. Those times when everything seemed okay, like there were no rules to follow, we could all do what we wanted at Shystee's. We could do Crystal or just smoke weed and do white. We got along with each other. I hit it with some of the guys there and once in a while with C.M., Jones wanted me to fuck him and when I wouldn't, at least he never went to people and bitched about it.

We watched some bad ass movies, and gettin' high would keep us awake all night and then Shystee would go over to his turntables in the main room and the beats were tight, dawg. Sometimes he wouldn't let us have anything to drink or wouldn't share his drugs. Even Jones started coming over and hanging around a lot and I laughed 'cause some of them thought he was a Narc 'cause he was fucking sober. And C.M. started bringing Esteban out of nowhere and even he started going to Shystee's. I mean, I think back to all this and I wonder, "How did the party end?"

Did I start all this the night I fucked Shystee in his bed with Ginger in the other room? I mean, maybe I shoulda done less drugs that night. Just weed and no coke? Something like that. 'Cause I got on him like a fucking lap dance and right next to us, Ginger was sitting there. And at the time I didn't think nothin' of it, 'cause I thought Ginger was just his fuck buddy, so why not go after him? And anyways, a lap dance like that alone doesn't automatically mean we're gonna have sex. I could even do something like that on Jones, and I was pretty damn sure I would never fuck Jones. So while I'm all rubbin' on Shystee, I look at Jones, who's already looking my way and I told him I loved him. And he looked down real sad and quietly said it back. A few minutes later, he left.

Later that night, some of us went to this bar and I sat at a table with Shystee, having drinks. At that point, I didn't know that Ginger was at the bar area, looking at us. You know, I think about this shit, and I can't understand why she let all this happen. She coulda some over and be like, "Get away from my boyfriend," or something. Or Shystee could have did the right thing and said, "Sorry, I can't do this." But with everything the way it is now, how can I think that Shystee could ever do the right thing. I really wanted to get laid with someone new that night, and I made Shystee my mark. I mean, I saw some kind of power in him, and that sounds fucked up with all the whining he did, but the way he seemed to make things happen, and for God's sake, I already fucked Adam, so Shystee was a step up.

I guess that when Shystee and me fucked in his bed later that night, Ginger saw us in the room, but again she didn't do anything. So when I told her later that I didn't know how serious their relationship was, I really meant it. You know, I may have my problems, but I ain't gonna go for someone that's taken. Shystee definitely ain't worth that much. And after me and Shystee hit it, them two didn't get back together as far as I know.

Man, if C.M. could understand just how sorry I was 'cause of what I did with Shystee. If I coulda had just a little more time to let him knew that I would do anything to make this all up to him. That day I went over there and told him I loved him, even that wouldn't have been good enough. I'm talking about showing him some kind of loyalty like I never did before. So that he would know for sure that he could trust me again, the trust I lost from him when I first started fucking around on him.

But he'd have to know. The whole total truth. Something that would be hard to hear. Something that would risk losing his friendship forever. 'Cause he already knows some of it, but not the most important part. The night soon after C.M. got clubbed, when Shystee came to see me at the club. C.M. was pissed that after I was s'posed to be on his side, here I was sitting on Shystee's lap for a long time. I told C.M. that I sat on Shystee's lap to find out why he attacked him. And Shystee was so nice and sweet that night, dawg. He admitted that crystal had him, dawg. That it made him think things was different from the way it really was. That he remembered seeing C.M. attacking Nice Guy and he honestly thought he had to save Nice Guy's life.

I never even told this part to C.M. because I knew he would say it's bullshit. But, anyway, we talked and I gave him a couple of dances. Then he said he had weed at the house he was staying at and it had been two days since I had anything, so I couldn't turn him down. So when we got there, we blazed, and of course, before you know it, we're naked at that apartment, I don't know where, and of course we did it and I got a cab out of there the next day.

So fine, I did this! I did something … I can't take back … Now that C.M.'s gone. I'm sure he knows right now, and I pray so hard that he made it to heaven. He was everything to me! Why couldn't I just tell him. Now I have to go the rest of my life with no more chances. No way to get this off my chest. I'm sorry! I'm so sorry, C.M. Why the fuck did you have to die. Why did you have to go to Nick and Adam's house. You knew you couldn't trust them.

Oh, my two boys are gone. I shoulda given you a chance, Jones. You were in love, you had feelings for me, but I was loving you, that was stupid, trying to save you.

*   *   *   *

So through all this, the only thing I can do is start over. So, since the day I heard the news, I have been leaning real hard on Miller, and he's been keeping me okay. He makes sure that everyday we spend together, we keep our minds on what we're doing and not get bored so I don't start thinking too much about the past. You know, we do some outdoor things, some indoor things. We went to the zoo, Miller's the only man I've ever been with that has actually offered to take me there. And there was Natural Bridge Caverns, those caves were bad ass. Schlitterbahn, the big water park, it was so beautiful. He took me to a lot of movies, a lot of the scary kind I like. And he took me to nice restaurants. You know, he made a good living and he told me he would take care of me as long a I needed, so for awhile I would dance only one or twice a week. Living with him made my life stable. I stopped living the way I was living, sleeping with a lot of men, but we smoked weed together and made love. I didn't think of getting with other men 'cause I was with Miller, I wanted this to work. I wanted for things to become simple, I didn't wanna think anymore, maybe just some other things like poetry.

I started writing poetry again, but it was different than it used to be. Before, I was talking about Johnny Depp and flowers and now I was thinking about everything I remembered about my boys, my two boys. Somehow the three of us had a connection that even now I couldn't explain. I could write about what they looked like, how they acted, how each one meant to me. How C.M. was a dark stallion and I was a princess an he would take me to far away meadow and change into a human when no one was around to see.

Jones was one of those guys who would go around doing good deeds for everyone in the village but nobody knew his name and where he lived. So I could talk about both, making them so beautiful in my mind and I never could figure out how I could be with both of them. But, really, all I had to do was go back to the memories. But then I would stop 'cause the memories would just make me start crying. And then Miller would come over to hug me and I just pushed him away 'cause there's no way that Miller could solve this. One of these times I cried the most, I told him to take to McDonald's so I could get an ice cream. When we got home, he asked to read my poems and I told him, "Only if you don't get jealous." And he said, "Why would I get jealous?" And I go, "Cause they're about me and my boys," real soft. And, of course, he knew what I was talking about, and while he was reading the poems quietly to himself, I fell asleep on the chair.

✳   ✳   ✳   ✳

3 Months Later

I guess it's been almost 6 months since my boys got killed. I started having Miller take me out to their graves about once a week for about a month now. It's kind of a bitch to see both because Jones' is at Ft. Sam Houston because his grandfather was an officer in the army and C.M.'s is on the west side. But there's no way I'm gonna complain about something like that.

When I come out to these graves, I leave a rose for each week's trip. So the first time I left one, the second time, two, and on and on. We spend maybe ten minutes at each grave and I say a prayer and then we stand there for awhile. This latest visit, the weather was cold so we didn't stay as long.

I wish I could make a decision about how long I will keep doing this. I wish I could say the rest of my life, but that might not happen. It's just natural after awhile, you'll forget or get lazy. Shit, I barely ever visit my own mom's grave anymore. So, I'll do this as long as I can. And I don't think this is some kind of obsession. They were close enough to me to deserve some visits. And yes, I had other friends that had nothing to with all this drama, but they're not around 'cause we lost touch over time or my relationship with Miller left time for other people. That's how it goes. Miller is much more important to me right now and honestly I don't need anyone else.

And you know what, I don't want these so-called "friends" anyway. 'Cause some of these I know, like Rose, are still on crystal. It's been a long fuckin' time since I did it, and I'm not about to hang out with one of these homies or homegirls and get addicted again. And someone could easily just look at Rose and tell how cracked out or whatever she is, like her sunken in face, like her teeth are going bad, and it looks like her body is going to break in half and I even think I would be strong enough to break her back. But I still don't care what anyone says, there is no excuse that it makes it okay. If you do all this crazy ass shit 'cause of the crystal and you don't remember what you did and someone tells you the next day, you need to think about not doing it again. You know, at least think about it. And, you know, it's not just Shystee, but some guys on drugs really wanna rape women or don't care about anyone but themselves. But, you know, weed is different. It's like, the worst thing that can happen is someone can trip out a little. But people can't even fight when they're stoned.

But, I can't see anyone do any hard drugs anymore. The party's over. Once someone gets killed, that's it. Someone has to do something to end these problems. I'd like to think I could help get this done. In fact I don't even know who I would help or who would help me. These guys are still around and I say guys 'cause I can't imagine how any of the girls could've been involved with killing my boys. Then again, Daisy loved taking both sides. Of course, how can I judge after what I've done. But I do know I have tried my hardest to pray to make up for what I did. Prayer on my own, going to church, visiting their graves.

Now I want to show what I really can do for my boys. Something that no one on this earth who knows me could ever believe in a thousand years. I guess I would have to approach Ginger and Daisy, but in different ways. Ginger is a nice, good girl, so if she knows anything she's not telling, it's cause she's scared and not trying to cover it up. But I'm pretty sure Daisy is hiding who did it, would love to keep this secret forever. I know she's talked to Shystee and I have the feeling Nice Guy's been around her also. So I just need to catch her by herself at her apartment, pull out my little knife and do what I need to do. To be honest, I don't need her knowledge of who did it, 'cause I already know where it happened. I just hate Daisy 'cause of her sneaking around. I feel I made up for what I did and someone needs to do it to her 'cause she won't do it herself.

So then my nex target would be Adam, cause he lives at the house where my boys were. And after all this time, why wasn't anyone charged with murder? I got word that they showed C.M was an intruder and Jones was armed, in his car. Well, fine, if that's the way thing are gonna be, I will do what I need to do.

So I can go to Adam's window and see if his new girlfriend is there, and if she's not, I'll have him bring me in his room and we'll hit it hard, dawg. And then I'm gonna guess that he won't wanna tell me what happened, so I will reach quick for my knife from my purse and to his throat. And then when he tells me, I'll slit him anyway cause he had his part in this. So then I'll know what I need to know and who I need to take care of.

And I understand there's some problems. How do I get away with this? I don't. Because I betrayed C.M. and Jones and C.M. died when they shouldn't have, the murderers will get away with this if I do nothing. For the first time in my life, I wanna give my life for others, to make up for al the selfish things I've done. What about Miller, I'd be cheating on him. I don't care, this has to be done and I can't reason with him.

So, basically, when I take care of Adam, I'll know the identities. And one person I'm pretty sure is involved is Shystee. And this person is what it's all about. Shystee. If he likes San Antonio so much, let's see how he enjoys himself. 'Cause I'll lay it on him, dawg. I'll suck on his cock so hard, he'll be sore as hell after. I'll ride him. I'll let him doggystyle. I'll give him three straight days of sex if I have to. But I always have my little knife around me somewhere, especially when he goes to sleep. Yes, I definitely know Shystee's involved. Six months later and these are my images in my mind. How much I just wanna kill and yell out at everyone. I don't ever wanna be nice anymore.

So Miller comes home from work on this beautiful morning. Not even that cold out. He says, "What's with that frown on your face?" And I said, "Oh, I just had some stupid nightmare. I don't remember it now."

"Well, if you don't remember it, forget you had one."

"You know, you should know by now that I stay in my moods."

"Baby, the sooner you practice, the sooner you can get over their deaths."

"Who says I should have to get over them?" And I never told Miller about that dream. It's not something he needs to know about. And actually, it was these things I thought of when I was partly awake. It was something that hit. I wasn't trying to think those things up. So what did I do?

I let it just go away, just like it came. I'm not gonna kill anyone, so I just decided to pray even more, mostly for myself. I prayed that I get right with God and stay right with God. And I knew I could start by staying true to Miller. Over the months I danced more, but I didn't hook up with the dudes anymore and I drove home right after work.

And I still visited my boys' graves, but not as often. Things would come up or I wouldn't have enough time, 'cause I always felt I had to see both their graves on the same day. But I never stopped crying. Every time I would beg God to make this not true, to give my boys back. And I had to take the wilted roses away that were there on the next trip and replace them with the fresh new ones that took their place on the new visit.

Me and Miller didn't have sex a lot, but mostly it was because I didn't want to. Talk about change in my life. But not having sex wasn't really about my sadness. It was about the way I looked at Miller. We grew together in a way that sex was not needed, and it was probably 'cause I started feeling closer to God. I was going to church a lot more and crystal was out of my life. Miller became the only friend I had 'cause I stopped talking to some of the others after some time.

I was afraid of making friends now, especially in a club. 'Cause that's where I met C.M. The way I looked at things now, I didn't want to risk losing anyone anymore, so I only allowed myself Miller. And I really needed him. I needed him forever.

*   *   *   *

So now it's New Years Eve and it's been a few weeks since I visited my boys. I went while it was still daytime and I brought a whole dozen roses for each one of them and I went to see both of them like I always do. I decided to see C.M. first and it felt like a special day to me so I placed the flowers on the grave and I kneeled and prayed, "Dear Lord, I'm praying 'cause I want to know he's in heaven, I want to know that he is in pure happiness with you. He meant so much to me and I can see him laughing 'cause things is okay.... Why? Why? Why can't I get over this? I can't keep thinking about this shit! Sorry, but, when's this gonna end? I wake up sad every morning, and coming here doesn't solve this. Sorry, Sorry, C.M., I don't mean this at you, Okay Lord, I'm leaving and I'll come back another time." So finally I went to Jones' grave and, of course, I'm already crying, tears in my eyes and just like at C.M.'s I put the roses on Jones' grave and kneeled down and began praying. "I feel like I'm finally ready to tell you Jones, even though you died a long time ago and I never told you while you were alive. 'Cause I didn't…. I didn't … uhh … think you were gonna die, dawg. I thought I had plenty of time and I wasn't ready anyway. And maybe, since you're in heaven, you already know what I'm gonna say, but I'm gonna tell you anyway. You mean the most to me. You even mean more to me than C.M. and I didn't just love you, I was in love with you. I never told this to anyone before, and I was trying to deny it to myself. Do you remember when I told you I wanted you with me in heaven? I meant it. I wanted to save you and now that you're gone, I wish I didn't do it. Maybe I deserved to lose you because I took you for granted … and do you remember that late night when we walked around Trinity University and Alamo Stadium and we held hands the whole time? I felt like my hand was melting in yours. Remember when we held each other and it seemed like for hours? You maybe didn't hear everything, but I told you that you meant everything to me and I would care about you forever, and I do. Why … (Sniffle) … Why did you have to fucking(Shout)…. die…. I can't fucking…. I can't…."

End of "Cruisin' Around SayTown"

978-0-595-47669-5
0-595-47669-4

Printed in the United States
99093LV00004B/415/A

9 780595 476695